CHARLIE BUMPERS vs.

THE REALLY NICE GNOME

CHARLIE BUMPERS vs.
THE REALLY NICE GNOME

Bill Harley

Illustrated by Adam Gustavson

PEACHTREE
PUBLISHERS

Published by
PEACHTREE PUBLISHERS
1700 Chattahoochee Avenue
Atlanta, Georgia 30318-2112
www.peachtree-online.com

Text © 2014 by Bill Harley
Illustrations © 2014 by Adam Gustavson

Design and composition by Nicola Simmonds Carmack

The illustrations were rendered in India ink and watercolor.

Printed in January 2014 by RR Donnelley & Sons in Harrisonburg, VA, in the United States of America
10 9 8 7 6 5 4 3 2 1
First Edition

Library of Congress Cataloging-in-Publication Data

Harley, Bill, 1954-
  Charlie Bumpers vs. the Really Nice Gnome / by Bill Harley; illustrated by Adam Gustavson.
      pages cm
  ISBN 978-1-56145-740-3 / 1-56145-740-X
  Summary: Charlie has looked forward to being in the fourth-grade play, but is not at all happy when Mrs. Burke assigns him the role of the Nice Gnome.
  [1. Theater—Fiction. 2. Schools—Fiction. 3. Behavior—Fiction. 4. Family life—Fiction. 5. Humorous stories.] I. Gustavson, Adam, illustrator. II. Title. III. Title: Charlie Bumpers versus the really Nice Gnome.
  PZ7.H22655Cgr 2014
  [Fic]—dc23
                            2013026218

To Michele Eaton, who helps us
keep it all together

Thanks to my insightful readers, Debbie Block, Michele Eaton, and Jane Murphy; to Linda and Irshad Hazue for their kind hospitality; and to Vicky Holifield, my very fine editor.

Contents

1

What's a Thespian?

"Are you ready, thespians?" Mrs. Burke asked. "Are your desks cleared?"

"Yes," we all answered.

"But Mrs. Burke," I asked, "what's a—"

"Charlie," Mrs. Burke said. "What's that on the floor?"

I looked down. Somehow my math sheet had fallen on the floor. There was a sneaker mark on it. I picked up the paper and stuffed it in my desk.

Mrs. Burke frowned and shook her head. "Okay, all of you thespians," she said, "please listen carefully."

"What's a thespian?" I blurted out.

"Charlie, have you forgotten Rule Number Four of Mrs. Burke's Empire?" she asked.

"Raise your hand," Samantha Grunsky hissed, poking my back with a pencil.

Having Samantha tell me what to do was annoying. But I still wanted to know the answer to my question, so I raised my hand. But Samantha's was already up and Mrs. Burke called on her.

"Yes, Samantha," Mrs. Burke said.

"I know what a thespian is," she said.

That figures, I thought. *She already knows everything.*

"It's an actor," Samantha said.

I looked back at her and she gave me one of her I-know-everything looks.

"That's correct," Mrs. Burke said, "and today I want to talk about our play."

I squirmed in my seat. Maybe she was going to give us our parts for the play. It was hard to sit still. I already knew the part I really wanted.

Every year, each fourth-grade class does a special project. Mrs. Ladislavski's class (everyone calls her Mrs. L.) designs an obstacle course for the whole school to run through. Ms. Lewis's class makes a special lunch with food from all around the world.

Mrs. Burke's fourth-grade class presents a play. Everyone comes to see it, even the parents. There are lights and costumes and props and everything.

Last year the play was *The Elephant's Surprise*, and it was pretty good even though the elephant's cardboard trunk fell off halfway through the play and Mrs. Burke had to come out and hold it up every time the elephant talked.

At first, I thought I wasn't going to like doing a play. My older brother Matt told me I would have to be a bunny or something, and I didn't want to be a bunny. Especially if Matt or someone else was going to make fun of me.

But then last week Mrs. Burke read us the play. It was called *The Sorcerer's Castle,* and it was great. Really great. There was a bunny in it, but it was stuffed, so I was safe there.

The part I wanted to play was the sorcerer. His name was Kragon. The Evil Sorcerer Kragon. Mwa-ha-ha-ha!

It was the best part in the play. And it was really the only part I wanted. But I knew four other boys wanted to be Evil Sorcerer Kragon, too. And two girls.

Only one of us would get it.

Mrs. Burke picked up a big stack of papers. "I'm going to hand out scripts that will be yours to keep," she said. "At the top of the first page I've stapled a piece of paper that says what your part is."

This was it! Now my legs were jiggling and I couldn't sit still. Even my hair was tingling.

I *had* to be the Evil Sorcerer Kragon. I knew

that I could do the part really well—if I just got the chance.

Please, please, please, please, please! I thought.

"Your first assignment," Mrs. Burke continued, "is to go through all the pages and mark the lines that are yours. Wherever you see the name of your character, underline that part."

Mrs. Burke started calling people to the front of the class to get their scripts. I sat on the edge of my seat, ready to jump up. If she was going in alphabetical order, I would be called soon, since my last name is Bumpers. But then I heard her call Cory Filkins, so she wasn't going alphabetically.

Boogers! I couldn't wait much longer.

The kids who already had their scripts started whispering about their parts. I thought I heard Cory say something about "Sorcerer,"

5

but then Manny Soares said, "Me, too," so I figured they were the Sorcerer's Assistants.

Finally, after a million years, Mrs. Burke called my name.

My heart was really beating as I walked up. She handed me my script. "This is a big part, Charlie," she said, smiling. "I know you can do it."

I nodded. This was a good sign. The Evil Sorcerer Kragon was a big part.

When I got back to my desk, I looked down at the piece of paper stapled to the top of my script.

I looked up at Mrs. Burke, then at the paper again.

There must be some mistake!

I checked to make sure this was my script. "Charlie Bumpers" was printed on the upper right-hand side of the paper.

"The Nice Gnome?" I said out loud. "I'm the Nice Gnome?"

2

I Am Ruined!

If I had to make a list of parts I did *not* want in *The Sorcerer's Castle*, the Nice Gnome would be at the very top. It wasn't just that gnomes are pudgy little guys with pointy hats or that gnomes remind me of one of the squishy plush dolls my sister keeps on her bed. I didn't want the part because the Nice Gnome is ridiculously nice. Everything he does in the play is nice. He helps the Prince and Princess when they get stuck in the swamp. He bandages up the Fox when his paw is hurt. He's always polite.

He's so good it makes your teeth hurt.

But the main problem with the Nice Gnome was this:

He was boring.

The Evil Sorcerer Kragon was the opposite of boring. He was a bad guy, but in a very funny way. I already knew how to do his evil laugh because I had practiced it in my bathroom at home, looking in the mirror and rubbing my hands together.

"Mwa-ha-ha-ha! Mwa-ha-ha-ha!"

Also, the Evil Sorcerer Kragon has absolutely the best lines in the whole play. When things go wrong for him, he shouts, "You horrible people! My plans are ruined! My dreams are ruined! I am ruined!"

I had practiced that part a hundred times. Or at least four.

But now Mrs. Burke had given me the part of the Nice Gnome. Why would she do that? I wasn't that nice and I didn't look like a gnome.

I looked over at Hector. He was reading his script.

"What part did you get?" I asked.

"I'm the Prince's Servant," he said.

I nodded. Hector was from Chile, where they speak Spanish, and English was his second language. He was good at it—but still kind of shy. I thought about asking him to trade parts, but I knew he wouldn't want to learn all the Nice Gnome's lines.

Because there were a lot of them.

And they were all dumb.

Mrs. Burke was still handing out parts, so I leaned over toward Josh Little's desk.

"What part did you get?" I asked.

Josh smiled. "The Slimy Snake of the Swamp."

That was an excellent part. If I couldn't be the Evil Sorcerer Kragon, I would have settled for the Slimy Snake.

"I got the Nice Gnome part," I said. "It has a lot of lines."

I wondered why Mrs. Burke hadn't chosen Josh Little for the Nice Gnome. He would be a perfect Nice Gnome. The truth was, Josh Little *was* a nice gnome. He was polite and did everything right. Except for the time he threw up on Mrs. Burke's desk, which was an accident because he was sick.

"I wish I was the Slimy Snake instead of the Nice Gnome," I said.

"Well, Mrs. Burke decided which parts we should have, so she probably has a good reason for giving you that part."

Exactly what a nice gnome would say.

Just then I heard Sam Marchand's voice. "Mwa-ha-ha-ha! My plans are ruined! My dreams are ruined. I am ruined!"

My stomach sank. Now I knew who the Sorcerer was.

And then it got even worse.

"Guess what?" Samantha Grunsky said to me. "I'm the Princess!"

I put my head down on my desk.

Boogers! It was my perfect nightmare!

The Nice Gnome spends most of his time *very nicely* helping the Prince and Princess get to the Sorcerer's castle. Which meant *I* was going to have to be nice to *Samantha Grunsky!*

I couldn't believe Mrs. Burke had made me

Samantha Grunsky's helper! Mrs. Burke was more evil than the Evil Sorcerer Kragon, who had kidnapped the Queen's Magic Talking Rabbit.

Before I could say anything, Mrs. Burke snapped her exploding fingers. Our teacher has the loudest fingers on the planet—they sound like miniature atomic bombs going off. Everyone got quiet. Alex McLeod, Mr. Crazy Legs, had been running around looking at everyone else's scripts, and even he scooted back to his seat.

"Alex," Mrs. Burke said, "if you get up one more time today, I'm going to chain you to your seat."

She was joking. I think. Mrs. Burke has a weird sense of humor.

"All right," she said. "Everyone has their parts. Please mark your lines tonight. Now it's time to get ready to go home."

I raised my hand. I wanted to ask her about changing parts. I'd take just about any other part but the Nice Gnome, except for the stuffed bunny. I'd even be one of the Mice in the Woods if I had to.

But Mrs. Burke just kept talking. "I worked hard to find good roles for everyone, and I want you to start learning your lines right away. People in the first scene, please try to have your lines memorized by next Monday. The rest of you, read over your parts. Stage crew, please go over the whole play so you know the scenes."

I still had my hand up.

"Do you have a question, Charlie?"

There was something about the way she asked that made me think this wasn't a good time. I lowered my hand and shook my head.

I was still the Nice Gnome.

3

The Call of Nature

On the bus ride home, I sat down next to my best friend, Tommy Kasten. My little sister Mabel (my dad calls her "Squirt," but I call her "the Squid") was sitting in the front of the bus with Tommy's sister Carla. Tommy and I aren't in the same class this year—he's in Mrs. L.'s class—but we're still best friends.

"I got the worst part in the play," I said.

"What is it?" Tommy asked. "The talking elephant? I hope they got a better trunk this year!"

"No. It's a different play. But a worse part. I'm the Nice Gnome."

"The Nice Gnome?" Tommy laughed.

"It's not funny! I wanted any part but that one. And I have to help the Princess. And guess who the Princess is?"

Tommy didn't have to guess. "Samantha Grunsky."

"Right! I really wanted to be the Evil Sorcerer Kragon, but Sam Marchand got that part."

"Evil Sorcerer. That sounds like a great part," Tommy said.

"It is! But I have to be the Nice Gnome."

"Do you have to look kind of tubby and wear one of those pointy hats and talk in a squeaky voice or something?"

"Probably," I muttered.

"Maybe you could change parts with someone."

"I don't know. Mrs. Burke said she worked hard to pick out the roles." I looked out the bus window and thought about my teacher. I liked Mrs. Burke, but she was really strict. "I know her.

She likes to do things her way."

"But couldn't you explain to her why you can't do the Nice Gnome part?" Tommy asked. "If you gave a really good reason, maybe she'd listen."

◆ ◆ ◆

When the Squid and I got home, Matt was already there—the middle school gets out earlier than ours. He was sitting at the kitchen table reading a magazine called *Gamer's World*. Matt's crazy about computer games and plays them all the time, even though Mom and Dad are always telling him to do something else.

Mom was still at work—she's a nurse who visits people at their homes. Dad usually got home right before supper.

I grabbed some cookies from the jar on the counter and collapsed onto a kitchen chair. I thought about what Tommy had said on the bus.

"Don't forget to walk Ginger," Matt said.

"I know," I said.

"You should do it now," said the Squid as she sat down across from me.

"You're not my boss, Mabel."

Ginger was already jumping around, eager to go out, but I didn't feel like doing it.

"It's your job," the Squid said. "Remember when we all agreed on our jobs?" Then she skipped out of the room.

I remembered. But we hadn't exactly agreed on them. Dad had announced that we all had to have special chores. Matt got to be in charge of carrying out the garbage cans and recycling bins and getting dinner started when Mom and Dad were going to be late. The Squid was in charge of setting the table and sweeping the kitchen and straightening the family room.

It was my job to feed Ginger twice a day and walk her every afternoon. Mom said since I begged the most for the dog, I should be the one to walk her. But it didn't seem fair that I had to do something that took more time than anyone else's job.

The Squid wanted a cat. Matt said he didn't want anything he had to take care of, unless it was a python. I'm not sure Mom and Dad wanted either a dog or a cat. But they definitely did not want a python.

Since I wanted a dog the most, I had to walk Ginger. Plus, Dad said I was old enough and the Squid wasn't.

I know Ginger is mainly my dog, and I like playing ball with her and having her sleep in my room. But it still didn't seem fair. Matt and the Squid played with Ginger sometimes, too. Shouldn't they have to walk her once in a while?

Instead of walking Ginger, I stomped into the family room and flopped down on the couch. I turned on the television, but then turned the volume down really low so no one would hear. *Buck Meson— Detective from Andromeda*, my favorite show, was just starting. I didn't get to see it very often, since Mom didn't want us to watch television during the week. But I figured I could see the first part and then walk Ginger.

Buck Meson is a superhero who came from another planet to solve mysteries on earth. He can do this great thing with his eyes—shoot beams of electrons at people so they drop whatever weapons they're holding. He never uses his power to hurt anyone, which is pretty amazing. I would think he might want to use his electron stare once or twice on some bad guy's rear end, just to teach him a lesson.

He has a bunch of great lines he says all the time. When the bad guys are about to do something really terrible, Buck always says, "I DON'T THINK SO!"

Then he does his electron stare.

It's pretty cool.

If only Mrs. Burke's play had someone like Buck Meson in it. Maybe she would have given me that part instead of the dumb Nice Gnome.

The *Buck Meson* theme song came on. It's this

sort of space rap and I know all the words by heart. I sang along:

> *Buck Meson! Standing tall.*
> *Buck Meson! He fights for all.*
> *Known in every nebula,*
> *Detective from Andromeda!*

I was only planning to watch a minute or two, especially since Ginger kept whimpering and licking my face. But then it got pretty exciting and before I knew it, Mom was standing in the doorway of the family room.

I don't think so...

"What are you doing?" she asked.

Trick question! No good answer.

"Uh…nothing," I said.

"Did someone walk Ginger?" she asked.

My mom can be like a lawyer destroying someone on the witness stand in court. Sometimes she asks one question after another and you answer without realizing she's proving you're guilty.

But I didn't have to answer this time because Ginger jumped on the couch, which she is not supposed to do, and started barking. She was dying to go outside. Ginger doesn't have to talk—you know if she's been walked or if she's eaten by how crazy she gets.

"I was going to do it in a few minutes," I said.

"Charlie! How long have you been home?"

Another trick question! She knew how long I had been home.

"It's your job to walk Ginger," she said, standing in front of the TV screen so I had to look at her.

"I know," I said.

Mom turned off the television. I hate it when she does that. "You know the rules about watching TV. Go walk Ginger now. Then do your homework."

"Mom, I can't do everything," I said.

"I don't see you doing anything except watching television," Mom said.

"Yeah, but—"

"No 'yeah buts,' Charlie. Walk Ginger. It's your job," Mom said. Then she turned and left so I couldn't argue or whine.

Boogers. Whining isn't any fun when there's no one there to hear you. And arguing with Mom when she was tired was a bad idea.

I went into the kitchen and put on my jacket. Matt was still sitting there reading.

When I took down the leash, Ginger started to chew and tug on one end. The leash is old and you have to make sure it snaps tight.

Ginger wouldn't hold still.

"No, Ginger!" I said. "No chewing!"

She jumped up and whirled around, tangling me up in the leash.

I finally got it untangled and snapped it on her collar.

"Have a good walk, Poopmeister," Matt said.

"Ha ha ha," I said, opening the door.

Ginger pulled the leash right out of my hand. She ran out into the yard and started running around in circles and barking.

"Ginger, come!" I yelled. But she just kept running around.

I put my fingers in my mouth and let out the special whistle I learned from my Uncle Ron during one of his visits. It's really loud. Uncle Ron is my dad's younger brother, and he knows all sorts of cool stuff.

Ginger ran over and I hooked her up again. As soon as I made sure I had a good grip on the leash, we headed down the driveway.

The minute we got to the street,

Ginger headed over to the curb and started sniffing. She'll sniff at anything. I tried to pull her back, but she dug in her paws and stretched her neck out and kept smelling around. There was nothing there—it was just a concrete curb, but she snuffled at it like it was a big piece of steak.

"Come on, Ginger!" I gave the leash a yank and she tore herself away from the yummy-smelling concrete. We'd only walked another ten feet when she started sniffing a little patch of grass on Mrs. Cohen's yard.

I waited a while, hoping Ginger was ready to do her business. I think you know what I'm talking about. When you walk a dog, you aren't just giving them exercise. You're actually taking them out to poop.

Mom doesn't like it when we say "poop." She says I should use the words "potty break." I am not using the words "potty break."

Dad calls it "answering the call of nature." I say it doesn't matter what you call it, it's still gross to watch. And even worse to clean up.

Ginger pulled and sniffed and finally peed next to the stop sign on the corner. One down, one to go.

Or Number One down, Number Two to go.

But there were other things I had to watch out for, too. Walking Ginger around the block is like trying to get through an obstacle course. Halfway around the block is this little yappy dog in a fenced-in yard. He belongs to Mrs. Lapidus, and his name is Lovey-Doodle.

I'm not kidding.

Lovey-Doodle throws himself at the fence and barks at Ginger like he wants to kill her. Ginger just goes up and wags her tail at him.

I can't stand Lovey-Doodle.

Then there are the two cats around the corner from Lovey-Doodle. They sit in the window and swish their tails back and forth and lick their fur and pretend like they don't notice Ginger, even though I know they do. Ginger's eyes bug out when she sees them and she pulls with all her might against the leash. I think she'd jump over the bushes and break right through the window if she had a chance. The cats seem to love it.

I hate it.

But in a way, the squirrels are the worst. The squirrels could be anywhere on the block, like little evil gremlins, waiting for us. If Ginger sees them, she tries to climb the tree and barks at the top of her lungs. The squirrels chatter back at her like they're laughing their heads off.

Then, finally, there's Mr. Gritzbach. Ginger loves Mr. Gritzbach, but he doesn't love Ginger. I try to keep her out of his yard.

Walking Ginger is like playing some kind of game where I have to defeat all my weird opponents to get to another world and then make it back home again. The Quest of the Poopmeister.

That day, when I turned the corner, I saw Lovey-Doodle wasn't out. That was good. I dragged Ginger by the house, and thought about the play.

I wished I could ask my mom to tell Mrs. Burke I

would make an excellent Evil Sorcerer Kragon. But I doubted Mom would do that. She'd probably like me being the Nice Gnome.

I figured my best bet was to find someone who really didn't want his part and then convince Mrs. Burke it was a good idea for us to trade.

We rounded the next corner. Ginger looked for the cats in the window, but they weren't there. Things were going great.

But when we turned the last corner and headed back toward our house, Ginger still hadn't, you know…answered the call of nature.

"Come on, Ginger!" I said. "Do something."

No luck. She just kept sniffing and snuffling and snorting and pulling.

We came to the Gritzbachs' house. This is a dangerous part of our walk, because there are so many things for Ginger to sniff.

Mr. and Mrs. Gritzbach love lawn ornaments. They have a little deer statue with one ear broken off, a fancy bench no one ever sits on, some little cartoon characters whose legs spin around when the wind blows, and some fake geese standing on the grass. Ginger wants to sniff all of them.

I tried to hurry on by, but before I even got to the Gritzbachs' front walkway, Ginger dragged me right into the middle of their yard.

She acted like she was thinking about pooping.

I looked up at the front porch. I didn't see Mr. Gritzbach anywhere. The garage door was closed, so I couldn't see if any cars were home.

I really didn't want Ginger to poop in their yard, but I really wanted her to do it *somewhere* so we could go home.

She started snuffling like crazy at a spot in the middle of the Gritzbach's lawn. Ginger sniffed and sniffed and then squatted in that shaky way she has. I wonder if it's kind of embarrassing to be a dog and have some kid standing there while you do what you have to do.

She answered the call of nature.

Then came the part I hated the most—the part

that makes you wonder why you ever wanted a dog.

I stuck my hand in the plastic bag like it was a glove and picked everything up and turned the bag inside out. Completely gross.

Charlie Bumpers—Poopmeister.

As I stood up, I saw Mr. Gritzbach standing on his doorstep, staring at me with his arms folded across his chest. Mr. Gritzbach is short and round and kind of old and doesn't have any kids.

"What are you doing?" he asked.

Trick question! No good answer! What did he think I was doing? I was standing there with Ginger's leash in one hand and a bag of poop in the other.

"Don't worry, Mr. Gritzbach!" I called. "It's all cleaned up."

Ginger wagged her tail and barked her friendly bark.

He frowned and shook his head slowly, then went inside and closed the door.

I pulled Ginger back onto the sidewalk. Once she was off the grass, she trotted straight to our house like it was where she'd always wanted to go.

I have to do this every day.

The Nice Gnome was so nice, he would probably love this job.

But I didn't want to be the Nice Gnome.

4

The Dumb Fox

"Hey, Sam," I said the next day on the playground. "I was counting up the lines and the Nice Gnome has a lot more than the Evil Sorcerer."

"So?" Sam Marchand asked.

Mrs. Burke was letting us run around for ten minutes before math. This was my chance to find someone who would trade parts with me. I'd decided to start with the part I wanted the most.

"I was just thinking that you'd be a really good Nice Gnome," I said. "You'd be great at remembering all the lines."

Sam shook his head. "No way. The Evil Sorcerer

Kragon is the coolest part. My mom said she'd make me a black cape with skulls on it. If I was the Nice Gnome, I'd probably have to wear a red pointy hat." He headed over to the side of the playground where some kids were playing soccer.

Boogers. Any kid whose mom was making him a cape with skulls on it would never want to trade parts with a gnome. Especially not if they had to wear a red pointy hat.

I'd have to find someone else.

I looked around. Alex McLeod was running back and forth like a madman. Manny Soares and Robby Rosen were throwing a ball against the side wall of the school. Manny was one of the Sorcerer's Assistants. I didn't really want that part—there were hardly any lines. But Robby Rosen was the Fox and had some funny things to say. I figured it was worth a try.

"Hey, Robby. What part are you in the play?" I asked, trying to sound like I didn't care.

"I'm the dumb Fox," Robby said. He threw the

ball and stepped aside so Manny could take his turn catching it.

"Yeah, it *is* a dumb part," I agreed. I waited until he threw again. "I'm the Nice Gnome."

He didn't say anything.

"Want me to trade with you?" I offered, like I was doing him a favor. "That way you wouldn't have the dumb Fox part and you'd have a lot more lines."

Robby didn't say anything. He just kept throwing that dumb ball at the dumb wall and didn't say anything about the dumb Fox. Or the dumb Nice Gnome.

"So, do you want to trade?" I asked again. "We could talk to Mrs. Burke about it."

Finally he caught the ball and stopped.

"No. The Gnome has too many lines. I wanted to be on the stage crew, moving stuff around. That would be more fun."

Boogers. That wouldn't help me at all.

Our time on the playground was running out. I looked around for someone else to trade with. Just as I turned my head, Alex flew by, nearly bumping into me. Then I got an idea.

"Alex! Alex!" I yelled. But he just kept running. The next time he ran by, I grabbed his arm.

"Alex, you're on the stage crew, right?"

"Yep," he said. He kept squirming and looking around. I felt like I was trying to hold onto a wild animal.

"Want to be the Nice Gnome? It's a big part."

"Sure!" he said. "That would be awesome! But who would be on the stage crew?"

"Don't worry, I've got it all figured out. If you'll be the Nice Gnome, which is my part now, then Robby will take your place on the stage crew. I'll be the Fox, which is his part, and everyone will be happy!"

"Okay with me."

"All right," I said. "Let's talk to Mrs. Burke when we get inside. You and me and Robby."

"Sure, okay," Alex said. Then he was off again, his crazy legs flying every which way.

I went back over to Robby and explained the plan.

"Great!" he said. "That way I won't have to learn any words!"

On the way back into the school, I said to Alex, "Why don't you talk to Mrs. Burke?" I figured it was safer for him to do the talking. Then it wouldn't look like this was all my idea.

◆ ◆ ◆

Back in the classroom, Mrs. Burke was writing some math problems on the board.

"Mrs. Burke?" Alex said.

She turned around and seemed surprised to see all of us standing there. "What is it, boys?"

I gave Alex a little tap on the arm to remind him he was supposed to talk. He started slowly, but then after he got going, he couldn't seem to stop.

"Umm, Mrs. Burke...you know...I mean... we had this idea about changing parts for the play because then I would get to be the Nice Gnome but you shouldn't worry because Robby would take my place in the stage crew and then since he couldn't be the…the…"

Alex stopped and looked at me. He had forgotten what part Robby was playing.

"The Fox," I whispered.

"The Fox!" Alex hopped from one foot to the other. "Robby was going to be the Fox but then he would have my part which isn't really a part and then I would have the Nice Gnome part because Charlie doesn't want that part either so he could be…he could be…"

"I could be the Fox if I had to," I said, like I was trying to help everyone.

"Right!" Alex said. "The Fox. See, Charlie's the Fox and then I'm going to be the Nice Gnome because Charlie wouldn't be it anymore when he was the Fox. And then Robby would do my part, the…the…"

"Stage crew," I said.

"Yeah!" Alex said. "The stage crew!" He smiled like he'd explained everything perfectly. Robby just stood there.

Mrs. Burke looked at Alex, then at Robby, then at me. I felt like she looked at me a little longer than anyone else.

"No," she said.

Then she went back to writing on the board.

"Because, Mrs. Burke—"

"No," she repeated without looking back. "Absolutely no trading parts."

5

The Squid is Persistent

First thing when I got home that afternoon, I walked Ginger. By some miracle she did her business right away. She didn't even stop when we passed the Gritzbachs' yard. When we got back, I hurried to my room and closed the door so no one would bother me. I opened my backpack and pulled out the script. I didn't take the time to mark my lines yet—I just looked at them all. There were even more than I'd thought, including a really long speech at the end.

Someone knocked on my door. "Hey, Charlie!" the Squid yelled.

"Go away," I said.

She opened the door a little bit. "What are you doing?" she asked.

"None of your business," I said, sliding the script under my backpack. "Go away."

She pushed the door open a little wider. "You were looking at something."

"Big duh," I said. "I'm busy."

"Busy doing what?" She opened the door all the way and stepped inside.

"Nothing," I said. "Please go away."

She peered at the corner of the script that was sticking out. "Is that the play? Carla said you told Tommy you don't like your part."

My best friend couldn't keep his mouth shut! I needed to tell him to quit telling Carla anything, since she would blab it to the Squid and the Squid would come in my room and bug me. "It's none of your business," I said. But she didn't listen.

"She said you told Tommy you're the Good Elf and you don't want to be the Good Elf. Why not?"

"It's not an elf. It's a *gnome*. I don't want to be it

and I don't want to talk about it and I don't want you in my room."

"Why don't you want to be a gnome? Is he mean?"

"He's not mean, he's *nice*. Now go find something else to do."

"I will if you tell me why you don't want to be a nice gnome."

"It's a dumb part and it's a dumb play."

"What's it about?"

"Mabel…"

My sister knew I meant business when I called her Mabel, which is her real name. She got this droopy look on her face and her lower lip started to quiver. "Just tell me," she whined, "then I promise I'll go."

The Squid never gives up. My dad says, "Mabel is persistent." Whatever she was, she wasn't leaving until I told her something. So I did.

"It's about this kingdom called Gorlandia. The King is sick, and the Prince and the Princess have to go rescue the Magic Rabbit who knows how to make the magic potion that will save the King. Now go."

"But what happened to the Magic Rabbit? Why does it have to be rescued?"

"It got stolen from them by the Evil Sorcerer Kragon."

"A sorcerer? Ooooh. Is *he* mean?"

"Yes, he's mean and he's scary. And I really wanted to be the Evil Sorcerer Kragon but I'm stuck with the Nice Gnome."

I had told the Squid a lot more than I'd meant to. She is very pestering and very sneaky in her six-year-old kind of way. Like Dad says, she is persistent.

"But what's wrong with the Nice Gnome? What does he do?"

"I told you enough. Go away."

The Squid sat down on the floor in front of my bed. "Pleeeezy pleeeeze? Just tell me what the Nice Gnome does and I'll leave."

41

"There's not much more to tell. The Nice Gnome helps the Prince and Princess get to the Sorcerer's castle. They go through the forest and then the desert and then the swamp, and in each place they meet some creature—a fox and a snake and a camel and an owl. Then they all go to the Sorcerer's castle, except the Nice Gnome, who says goodbye and doesn't even get to go see the Evil Sorcerer Kragon."

"That still sounds like a good part to me. He sounds like a really, really nice gnome."

"He is and I hate him. Now please get out."

"You're not supposed to say 'hate.' And anyway, why do you hate him if he's nice?"

"Mabel!" I yelled at her because she was being really annoying. "Get out *now!*"

I yelled too loud I guess, because the next thing I knew Matt had stuck his head in the door. I could see right away that things were going to get worse.

"Charlie, you shouldn't yell at your little sister," Matt said.

"She's in my room and I told her to get out. You don't let *me* come in *your* room."

Matt squatted down and looked into the Squid's face. "Why is he yelling at you, Mabel?"

"Because he doesn't like his part in the play," she said.

Matt smiled his evil grin. "Why, is he a bunny?"

"No, I'm not a bunny! Both of you get out!"

"He's got a good part," the Squid said. "He's a gnome. A really, really nice gnome."

"A gnome?" Matt said. He started to laugh. "You mean a guh-nome? A guh-nice guh-nome?"

"No, just a gnome," the Squid said. "A nice gnome. Anyway, you don't say it 'guh-nome.'"

"Gnome begins with the letter *g*, Mabel," Matt explained like he was a teacher or something. "The *g* is silent, but I think it sounds more appropriately dorky if it's pronounced 'guh-nome.'"

"That doesn't make sense," the Squid said. "But I like gnomes and dwarfs and things like that. I wish I could be a nice gnome in the play."

"Guh-nome," Matt said.

"Guh-nome!" the Squid repeated, laughing.

"Get out of my room!" I shrieked. "Both of you!"

"Okay, okay!" the Squid said. "You don't have to scream at us."

"You're not being a very guh-nice guh-nome," Matt said. "Come on, Mabel. Let's leave the guh-not guh-nice guh-nome by himself."

When they were gone, I shut the door again.

Now I hated the Guh-nice Guh-nome even more.

6

The Magic Rabbit of Gorlandia

The next Monday morning, Mrs. Burke held up a handout. "Listed on this sheet are all the things you are responsible for regarding the play," she said. "Besides knowing your lines, you are also responsible for assembling or making your costumes. Please show this to your parents so they can help you. And remember, if you ignore your responsibilities, you will be hunted down by my secret police." She gave us one of her smirky smiles.

Mrs. Burke had this really weird sense of humor. Sometimes it was hard to tell if she was kidding or not.

I tried to imagine police coming into the classroom and arresting kids for not learning their lines.

"Sarah and I are meeting at my house to make the camel," Tricia Davidoff said. She was the front of the camel, and Sarah Ornett was the rear.

I would even rather be the rear of the camel than the Nice Gnome, I thought.

"My mom's making a cape," Sam Marchand said. "With skulls on it. Mwa-ha-ha-ha!"

Everybody laughed. Except me.

"Next week, the stage crew will be painting the set with Ms. Bromley in art class. We'll also need help with props," Mrs. Burke went on. "Does anyone have any items we can use in the play?"

A bunch of hands went up. Some kids offered to bring in big cardboard boxes that could be made into rocks and trees and the Evil Sorcerer Kragon's castle. Candy Carlofsky had a magic wand that the Evil Sorcerer Kragon could use. Trevor offered to bring in a recording of spooky sounds that would be perfect for the swamp scene.

"Now," Mrs. Burke said, "does anyone have a stuffed toy rabbit we can use as the Magic Rabbit, and a cage we could put it in?"

Several kids raised their hands and started talking at the same time. Crystal Medeiros, who never speaks up in class, raised hers slowly.

"Yes, Crystal," Mrs. Burke said. "Do you have one?"

"I have a real rabbit," she said.

Everyone got quiet all of a sudden and looked at her. A real rabbit!

"Is it your pet?" Mrs. Burke asked.

Crystal nodded. "I share it with my brother."

Mrs. Burke smiled. "That's very kind of you to mention, Crystal. But I think it would be a lot easier to use a toy bunny."

Everyone started talking at once again.

"No! Please let us have a real rabbit for the Magic Talking Rabbit!"

Alex hopped around his desk like he was a rabbit himself.

"Please, Mrs. Burke," Ellen Holmes said. "A real rabbit would be great."

Mrs. Burke looked at Ellen. She was smart and everyone listened to her. We all trusted Ellen.

"I don't know," Mrs. Burke said. "I don't have much experience with real rabbits. Do you think it's a good idea, Crystal?"

Crystal nodded again. "I asked my dad if I could bring him in for the play and he said as long as Killer stays in his cage, it's okay."

"Killer?" everyone said at once. "Your rabbit is named Killer?"

Crystal smiled. "Yeah. My brother named him that because it was funny, since he's so gentle and quiet."

Killer, the Magic Rabbit of Gorlandia. It was an excellent idea.

We all looked at Mrs. Burke, waiting.

"All right," she said finally. "We'll try it."

We all cheered.

Crystal raised her hand again.

"Yes, Crystal?"

"I think we can only bring him in for one dress rehearsal. And we have to be very careful with him."

"Or else he'll kill us!" Cory shouted.

"Killer! Killer! Killer!" Alex chanted.

Mrs. Burke snapped her fingers for everyone to get quiet. But she was smiling. "The Killer Rabbit of Mrs. Burke's Empire!"

I smiled, too. I told you our teacher had a weird sense of humor.

KILLER

7

That's Ridiculous

When we got off the bus, it was starting to rain. I pulled my coat over my head and ran.

"Wait!" the Squid yelled. "You're supposed to walk with me!"

"Run!" I called back.

When I opened our back door, Ginger barked like crazy and jumped up on me. I pushed her out of the way so the Squid could get in. We took off our jackets and hung them on the hooks to dry.

Matt was sitting in the kitchen. He had made eight little cheese-and-cracker sandwiches and lined them up next to his magazine. "Mom told me to remind you to walk Ginger. She had to go visit someone and won't be home until right before supper. You guys each get two cookies."

I dumped my books on the table and sat down. I didn't feel like walking the dog because it was raining and I was too grumpy.

"What's with you?" Matt asked.

"I had a crummy day." I knew better than to complain about the play to Matt. He'd just bug me about my part.

"I got a star sticker when I read out loud." The Squid stuffed a cookie in her mouth. "I had a good day."

"I didn't," I said.

"Can I have one of your cookies?" the Squid asked. She was already eating her second one.

"No," I said. "You had two and I have two. It's equal and fair."

"You better walk the dog now, before you forget," Matt said.

How could I forget? He was telling me about it every thirty seconds!

"Why can't *you* do it today?" I asked.

"Can't," he said. "Too busy."

"Doing what?" I asked.

"Being a genius," he said.

"I *always* have to walk the dog," I said.

"That's because it's *always* your job." Matt didn't look up from his magazine.

"I still think you should do it sometimes," I said to Matt.

"I'll walk Ginger!" the Squid said.

"You're too little," Matt said, still looking down at *Gamer's World*. "Ginger pulls too hard."

"I'm bigger already," the Squid said. "Mrs. Diaz says when you're six you grow in your sleep. "

"Please, Matt," I begged. "Just this once?"

"Okay," he said. "I'll do it."

"You will?" I asked. I couldn't believe it.

"Sure," he said. "If you pay me." Then he grinned his evil older brother grin.

"How much?" I was suspicious, but if it was a quarter or even fifty cents, it might be worth it.

"Five dollars." He gulped down one of his cheese-and-cracker sandwiches.

"Five dollars! That's ridiculous!" I said.

"Then I guess you'd better walk her yourself."

"I'll do it for a quarter," the Squid said.

"Give it up, Charlie," Matt said. "It's your job."

Boogers.

I grabbed a plastic bag and shoved it into my pocket.

"Have a great walk, Charlie Poopsters," Matt said.

"Ha ha ha," I said.

"Can I have your other cookie?" the Squid asked.

"No. Leave it for me!"

It was raining even harder now, so I put on my raincoat and pulled the hood over my head. I snapped the leash on Ginger's collar, and she jerked me out the door.

She pulled me down the back stairs, straining at the leash and sniffing at everything along the driveway. Her tail was wagging about 200 miles an hour. Ginger was in dog heaven. I tugged on her

leash, but she wouldn't stop dragging me along.

"Ginger, no!" I said.

But then she stopped suddenly and squatted right there in our front yard!

I'd never had a bag of poop to hold so early on the walk. I had to hold it in one hand and Ginger's leash in the other.

I almost turned around right there, but I knew it wouldn't be fair to Ginger since she'd been inside all day, so I kept going even though I was getting really wet.

Things went great for a while.

Lovey-Doodle wasn't in the yard.

The cats weren't in the window.

But just as we got to Mr. Gritzbach's house, a big gust of wind whistled through the yard and sent the little cartoon characters' legs spinning around. Ginger barked at them like they were going to attack us.

"No, Ginger! No!" I pulled her away, but she wouldn't stop barking at the evil cartoon pigs and cats.

The front door opened and Mr. Gritzbach stepped out on the porch. When Ginger saw him, she shut up and started wagging her tail.

Mr. Gritzbach stared at us.

I held up the plastic bag, dripping with rain. "Don't worry!" I called. "Ginger's already answered the call of nature."

He shook his head and went back inside.

When we got home, Matt and the Squid were still sitting at the kitchen table.

"See?" said Matt. "That wasn't so bad."

The cookie plate was empty.

"Squid!" I yelled.

"I couldn't help it!" she squeaked.

8
I Hope There's Nothing Dead in It

After dinner a couple of days later, I was doing my homework at the kitchen table. My mom started to go through my backpack. "Charlie, this backpack is a rat's nest," she said. "I hope there's nothing dead in it."

I didn't say anything. Who knows? Maybe there was.

"What's this?" She pulled out the script of the play.

Boogers. I forgot I'd left it in there.

The staple had come out of it, and the pages

were already kind of wrinkled.

"Is this the play you're going to do?" She sounded excited.

"Uh-huh," I said.

"Oh, Charlie, this is just great. You're really going to like being in a play."

I didn't say anything. I knew that my mom had been in some plays when she was in college. Once she recited a whole speech to us that she still remembered from acting in a summer theater. That was a long time ago, before she went to nursing school.

Maybe *she* liked plays and having to memorize a million lines for the worst role ever, but *I* didn't.

"I always loved opening night," she said. "It's so thrilling."

"What if you didn't like your part?" I asked. "Was it fun then?"

"Sure. I just liked being out on the stage no matter how small my role was. You'll enjoy it, too. Working together on something is always fun."

I doubted that.

She looked at the note that had been stapled to the script. "Ah, I see you're the Nice Gnome. That sounds like a good part."

I didn't say anything.

Mom leafed through the script. "This is a big part, Charlie! You have a lot of lines!"

"Too many lines," I said. "And all of them are dumb."

She gave me a look. "What do you mean?"

"I just don't like the Nice Gnome," I said. "He's...um...

boring." I wanted to say stupid, but that would have been a stupid idea, because Mom doesn't allow us to say stupid.

"You're being silly," she said. "This looks like a great part."

"I'm not sure if it's going to be my part," I said. "It might change."

"Why is that?" she asked.

"Sometimes," I said, searching my brain for a decent answer, "sometimes...I mean...maybe Mrs. Burke will decide to change things."

She frowned. "I don't think you should plan on that."

"It could happen," I said.

"Well, it's better to start learning your lines right away," she said. "If you memorize your lines early, then you can

relax during rehearsals and have more fun. I'll tell you what. Finish up your other homework and we can read through the play before bedtime."

Once Mom gets an idea in her head, she's like a little dog that bites down on your pants leg and won't let go. She's almost as persistent as my sister.

Escape was impossible.

So when I finished my homework, Mom and I sat at the kitchen table and went through the script. I read my lines, and she read all the others. We got to the part in the forest where the Prince and Princess are lost and the Nice Gnome finds them and helps them. Mom read Samantha's line: "Who are you, kind sir?"

Unfortunately, that was the exact moment when Matt came into the kitchen looking for a snack. Or maybe just to bug me, which seems to be his job.

"I am the Nice Gnome," I read, "and I have been looking for you."

Before my mom could read her line, Matt said,

"The Guh-nice Guh-nome? The really Guh-nice Guh-nome? Looking for me?"

"Mom!" I said, turning to her for help.

"Matt!" Mom said. "Stop it."

"I am the Guh-nasty Guh-nome, and you cannot find me," he said. Then he grabbed a handful of pretzels and slipped out the door. Matt had ruined our practice session, but Mom made me keep going until we got through the whole script. It took forever and made me hate the Nice Gnome even more.

"Good job," Mom said when we finished. "I think I'll ask Mrs. Burke to e-mail me a file of the whole play, so we both can have scripts when we practice together."

"Mom!" I moaned.

"And you'll do a great job in the play. You have a big part. You just need to say your lines with more expression."

"I don't want this part," I said. "I don't want to learn these dumb lines."

"If you don't learn your lines, Charlie, everyone else in the play suffers."

I'm the one who is suffering, I thought. *Because I'm the dumb Nice Gnome.*

9

Would You Like Some Fries with That?

The next Tuesday, I sat with Tommy in the cafeteria. Hector took a seat at our table. He reached into his back pocket and pulled out his folded-up script. He opened it and stared at the top sheet.

"What are you doing?" Tommy asked.

"Trying to learn my part," Hector said. "I'm not very good at it. I keep making mistakes."

He was the Prince's Servant. He mostly just follows the Prince around and says, "Yes, Your Highness" or "No, Your Highness," except at the end when he reminds the Prince and Princess they have a Fox that can answer riddles.

"We'll help," I said. "I'll read the Prince's part and Tommy will read the Princess's part." I sort of knew the Prince's part already, since I'd been over the play so many times.

"Hey, wait a minute," said Tommy. "I don't want to be the Princess."

"And I don't want to be the Nice Gnome," I said. "At least you don't have to be one onstage."

We started practicing, with Tommy reading the Princess's lines in his sports announcer voice.

It took us a while to get through the whole scene because we were laughing so much. By the second time around, Hector remembered most of his lines. After two more times, Hector got every single line right. By the time we finished, I knew the Prince's part, and also the Fox's.

"You know what?" Tommy said. "This play would be a lot better if you said funny things."

"Like what?" I asked.

"Oh, I don't know. Like when the Prince says, 'Please bring my pillow so I can sleep,' the servant could say, 'Would you like some fries with that?'"

I laughed out loud. "That would be hilarious! People would love it!"

Hector smiled and shook his head. He was too shy to do anything like that. But it gave me an idea.

"Hey," I said. "If I'm stuck with this part, maybe I could at least change some of my lines so they would make people laugh. Mrs. Burke is too busy to change anything. But I could do it."

"You could be the Hilarious Gnome!" Tommy said.

"Exactly!" I said.

"Hey!" Tommy said. "Maybe you could use some lines from *Buck Meson—Detective from Andromeda!*"

I looked at Tommy and we both said at the same time, "I DON'T THINK SO!"

We cracked up. Anyone who'd seen *Buck Meson* on TV would laugh their heads off.

Hector shook his head. He took off his glasses, wiped them with his shirttail, then put them back on. He always does that. It's like he thinks if he cleans his glasses, the things he's looking at will make more sense. But when he put them back on, I could tell he thought Tommy and I were still as crazy as ever.

"I think you'd better ask Mrs. Burke," Hector said.

"Yeah," Tommy said. "But don't ask her until you can show her the new lines. That way she'll see how great it is."

"Okay," I said. "I just hope I can do it. It'll be a lot of work to rewrite all those lines."

"It's going to be easy," Tommy said, "because I'm going to help you, and I am a genius."

"You are a bozo," I said. "But if you're trying to be funny, that's better than being a genius."

Hector cleaned off his glasses again. But no matter how many times he did it, he was still going to look up and see two bozos.

10

Charlie Bumpers! Criminal!

As I walked in the back door that afternoon, Ginger jumped up on me. "Down, Ginger," I said. "Down!"

"Walk the dog," Matt said. He didn't even look up from his comic book.

"Would you please walk Ginger?" I begged. "Just today?"

"Sorry, I can't," he said.

"Please? Tommy's coming over and we need to work on the play."

"I have to finish this story. It's very important for my education."

"It's a comic book!" I yelled. "It's not part of school!"

"It's still important," he said. "It's about how zombies can turn back into living people, and I need to read it so I can help you become human again."

"Matt, please!"

"Sorry, Poopmcister!"

"I'll walk Ginger," the Squid said. "You only have to pay me a quarter."

I wondered if she could do it.

"I'm bigger than I was yesterday," she said. "Remember what Mrs. Diaz said? When you're six you grow in your sleep. So I'm definitely bigger."

"It's Charlie's job," Matt said.

"If she really wants to do it—"

"No!" The way Matt looked at me, I knew he meant it. He wasn't even being mean. "It's *your* job, Charlie."

Ginger started barking. Then she jumped up on me again.

It was no use.

I took the leash off the hook, but the Squid grabbed it out of my hand. "Let me do it," she said. "I know how." She tried to snap the leash onto the collar, but Ginger kept squirming around.

"Here," I said. "You have to be patient because sometimes it doesn't snap on all the way. Ginger, sit!"

Ginger sat, quivering all over. She couldn't wait to go for a walk.

I showed the Squid how to snap on the leash. "See?"

"I already knew that," she said, holding up the leash. "Can I walk her?"

"No," Matt said.

"Can I come with you?" she asked me.

I wished Matt would mind his own business. "Forget it, Mabel," I said. "It's my job. I'll do it myself."

"Okay," the Squid said. "But I know how to do it."

I opened the door. Before I could take the leash from my sister, Ginger pulled it from her hands and bounded out into the backyard. I stood on the porch and whistled and she came hurtling back.

"I can do that, too," the Squid said. She stuck her fingers in her mouth and blew. Nothing came out but a whooshing sound.

"Come on, Ginger," I said.

I walked her down the street, then turned at the end of the block. Up ahead was Lovey-Doodle's yard. I didn't hear any yapping. As we got closer, I saw Mrs. Lapidus on the sidewalk, looking up and down the street.

"Lovey-Doodle! Loooooovey!" She clutched her hands in front of her chest. "Lovey-Doodle, come!"

Mrs. Lapidus spotted me and Ginger. "Have you seen Lovey-Doodle?" she asked.

"No," I said. "I mean, I've seen it—him—but not today."

"It was such a pretty day, I let him out. I guess the gate wasn't closed." She looked down the street again. "I'm afraid he'll get lost. He never leaves the yard."

I felt sort of bad for her. I would hate losing Ginger. "I'll look," I said.

"Would you?" Her face brightened.

"Sure," I told her. "I'll look while I'm walking my dog around the block."

"That's so sweet of you, Charlie," she said, patting my arm. "I'll stay here in case he comes home."

Just as she said that, we heard a faint yapping noise coming from around the corner. We looked at each other.

"I think that's him," I said.

"I do, too!" she answered.

I gave Ginger a tug and started down the street. In about half a second, she was ahead of me, pulling on the leash.

We forgot all about pooping. Ginger didn't know where we were going, but she loved chasing things.

The yapping got louder and louder.

We turned the corner and saw him—Lovey-Doodle was yelping and howling in front of the window where the two cats were sitting like always.

Every once in a while, the little dog would run around underneath the bushes, then throw himself at the house like he was attacking a fortress.

The two white cats stared down at him like they were watching an animal at the zoo.

But then I noticed that the screen had fallen off the window.

There was nothing between the cats and Lovey-Doodle.

Ginger barked and pulled on the leash until she was standing up on her hind legs. I held on like I was riding a bucking bronco. She strained and gasped for a second, and then all of a sudden, the snap on her collar unhooked. She took off, leaving me holding an empty leash.

When Ginger realized nothing was holding her back, she lowered her head and headed for the window. About three feet from the bushes she leapt into the air, straight toward the cats.

Lovey-Doodle froze.

You'd think a cat being chased by a flying dog

would run under a couch or spring up onto a shelf somewhere out of reach. That would be the smart thing to do if you were a cat.

But instead of leaping back into the house, these cats jumped out the window and sailed over the bushes.

Ginger, amazed to find out she could fly, landed on top of the bushes. She struggled for a moment, then fell back onto the grass.

The cats screeched, raised up their backs, then scampered away. Lovey-Doodle came back to life and set off after them, yapping louder than ever. Ginger scrambled to her feet and ran after Lovey-Doodle.

I don't think those cats had ever been outside before. They ran around in crazy circles for about fifteen seconds with Lovey-Doodle and Ginger right

behind them,
and then
both cats
shot up a
tree. The
dogs bounded over and
started throwing themselves
at the trunk, still yowling at the
top of their lungs.

The cats crawled up four or five branches, then
stopped.

There were two squirrels right next to them.

The squirrels must have been surprised to see
two cats coming up after them.
But instead of climbing higher,
they scurried down the trunk
of the tree. Right toward
Ginger and Lovey-
Doodle.

The dogs were going nuts. They'd never seen squirrels running *toward* them. The squirrels scooted on by and ran down the street.

Ginger and Lovey-Doodle stopped barking for a second.

Lovey-Doodle looked at the squirrels, then started barking like crazy at the cats again.

Ginger looked up at the cats, then started chasing after the squirrels. They ran across the street into a neighbor's yard. There were no trees there, so the squirrels just kept going.

"Come, Ginger!" I yelled. Without even looking back at me, she ran past a big brick house and disappeared.

I was going to chase Ginger, but I remembered I'd promised Mrs. Lapidus I would help her. Her dog was right in front of me. And I had a leash.

Just as I hooked Lovey-Doodle to the leash, the door to the house with the cats flew open. A woman in a jogging suit rushed out.

"What's going on?" she shouted from the porch.

"Where are Alice and Gertrude?"

Alice and Gertrude? Why does everyone on this block have such weird names for their pets?

I just stood there, looking up in the tree. She hurried over and looked up, too. Her cats hissed at me and Lovey-Doodle.

"Did your dog chase Alice and Gertrude up there?" she shrieked. "Why didn't you stop him?"

It was way too complicated to explain. I didn't even know how to start. So I just said, "I don't know."

"Take your dog away from here right now," she said. "If I can't get them to come down I'll have to call the police."

Charlie Bumpers! Criminal!

"I'm sorry," I said.

"You should be," she said.

I thought about telling her it wasn't my fault that her screen came off, but I knew that when adults are mad, they don't listen very well. I got about ten steps down the sidewalk toward my house before

I remembered I was walking Lovey-Doodle, not Ginger. And I was going the wrong way. I had to turn back and go by the angry cat woman again.

"What are you doing?" she asked. I guess she thought I was crazy.

Maybe I was.

"I don't know," I said, hurrying past.

When I turned the corner, I started running.

Mrs. Lapidus was coming toward us. "You found him! You found him! Oh bless you, Charlie!"

When Lovey-Doodle jumped up on her leg, she picked him up and held him like a baby. "My little Lovey-Doodle-oodle-doodle," she cooed.

The snuggling and baby talk was pretty weird, but Mrs. Lapidus was so happy, it was okay.

I took the leash off and headed down the street. I

still had to find Ginger. Who knew where she was and what she was doing?

"Thank you, Charlie!" Mrs. Lapidus called.

"You're welcome!" I shouted. I jogged back the other way, because I didn't want to go by the cat lady's house again.

I rounded the corner and ran toward our house. Ginger was sitting on our front steps, waiting for me like nothing had happened. She had answered the call of nature right in front of my mom's flower bed. I picked up the mess with the plastic bag and took Ginger inside.

Tommy's mom had dropped him off and he was in the kitchen waiting for me.

"What took you so long?" he asked.

11

A Keg of Root Beer

I knew my mom had saved the script file from Mrs. Burke to the computer desktop. I opened it, then put Tommy in charge of typing up our changes. He's faster than I am.

I flopped down on the floor and propped my feet up on a chair. I needed a second to recover from the Lovey-Doodle and Alice and Gertrude dog-walk disaster. Ginger trotted over and started licking my face. For her, it had been the best walk ever.

Tommy scrolled through the script. "Okay," he said. "Here's a good place to start. The Princess—"

"Samantha Grunsky," I interrupted.

"Right, Samantha and you and the Prince and their servants are stuck in the desert. And you're running out of water. The Princess says, 'I'm so thirsty, I can't go on.' Then you, the Nice Gnome, say—"

"Don't call me the Nice Gnome, please," I said. "Call me the Hilarious Gnome."

"Whatever," Tommy said. "Your line goes like this: 'Just one cup of water would save our lives.' What do you want to say?"

I thought for a second. "Just one glass of root beer?"

"What about one *keg* of root beer? That would be funnier."

"Excellent," I said. "Type that in before we forget it."

We worked at the computer for over an hour and came up with some great new lines for the Gnome. The part was seven hundred times better.

We managed to put in "I DON'T THINK SO" four times. Every time it got funnier.

"Okay," Tommy said. "We're almost done. They just have to get to the castle."

"I know what I'm going to say when the Nice Gnome leaves. Instead of goodbye, I'll say, 'I have to answer the call of nature.'"

Tommy frowned, like he wasn't so sure about that line.

"Just type it," I said. "It's funny."

We finally finished. I think I'd worked harder at changing those lines than I ever had on any homework. I got up and stared at the computer screen. Our rewrite looked really official.

Mrs. Burke always said she appreciated hard work.

"Tommy," Mom yelled from the hallway, "your mother just honked. She's out front."

"Okay, Charlie," Tommy said. "All you have to do now is print this out and take it in." He put on his jacket and gave me a high five.

I walked with him to the door. "Thanks, Tommy. I think you just saved my life."

"No problem." He made a thumbs-up sign as he got into his car.

When I went back into the family room, my mom was looking at the computer screen.

"What's this?" she asked.

"The play," I said.

"What are you doing with it up here on the screen?"

"Nothing."

"How could it be nothing?" she asked.

Trick question! No good answer! I didn't say anything.

But now she was scrolling through the pages. Unfortunately for me, Mom knew the play pretty well.

"Charlie," she said. "The Nice Gnome doesn't say these things. There's nothing about root beer in the play."

I still didn't say anything.

"What are you and Tommy up to?"

"We're just changing a couple of things. To make it better."

"Does Mrs. Burke know about this?"

"I'm going to show her tomorrow."

"You know, Charlie, directors don't like it when actors change their lines."

"Mrs. Burke doesn't have time to change things, so I'm helping her."

"Charlie, this isn't a good idea. You'd better talk to her about your part if you're unhappy with it."

"I'm more than unhappy with it," I said. "I can't stand it."

My mom twisted her mouth up and stared at me for a few seconds. "Charlie, this is the part you have been given. It's time for you to quit whining and make the best of it." Then she left before I could say anything.

After I heard her go upstairs, I printed the new script. When it came out of the printer, with the paper new and smooth and the printing neat and clear, I thought it looked like a much better play. I just hoped Mrs. Burke would agree with me.

12

I Don't Think So!

The next day when we were getting ready to rehearse, Mrs. Burke broke us up into groups of four. Alex and Dashawn were in my group. So, unfortunately, was Samantha.

"Your job today is to help each other with your lines," Mrs. Burke said. "Everyone will take turns reading the lines before and after your partners', so each person can practice."

"I don't have any lines," Alex said.

"You can read the other parts in the scene," Mrs. Burke said.

I was glad Dashawn and Alex were in my group.

Reading with them would give me a chance to try out my new lines before I showed them to Mrs. Burke. "I made some changes," I said, holding up my new script. "So just keep reading, even if it seems different."

"You're not supposed to make changes," Samantha said.

"Let's just try it," I said. "You'll see. It's a lot better."

It was. When we got to the place where the Prince and Princess and their servants and the Nice Gnome meet the Fox in the woods, Alex spoke the Fox's words: "My paw is stuck in the trap. I can't get it out."

I read my new line: "Well, why'd you put it in there?"

Alex cackled and jumped up and down. "That's funny!"

"It *is* sort of funny," Dashawn said.

"It's not right," Samantha said. "And it's *not* funny."

I ignored her. We kept reading.

When we met up with the snake, Alex said, "Sssssssssweeeeeet to meeeet youuuuuu."

I read, "I DON'T THINK SO!"

Dashawn laughed again.

"Buck Meson!" Alex guffawed. "Awesome!"

I grinned.

Samantha folded her arms and frowned. "This isn't right. You're spoiling the whole play."

"I think it's better!" Alex said.

"So do I," said Dashawn.

"You'd better stop it," Samantha said.

Finally we got to the part where they were stuck in the desert. Samantha said her line: "I'm dying of thirst."

I read, "Just a keg of root beer would save our lives."

Dashawn laughed out loud. Alex hopped around, whooping.

Samantha stood up and raised her hand. "Mrs. Burke! Mrs. Burke!

Charlie's ruining the play!"

Mrs. Burke came over to our desks. "What's going on?" she asked.

"He's changing everything!" Samantha said. "He's trying to be funny, but he's not."

"It is funny, Mrs. Burke," Alex said, stopping to catch his breath. "It's really funny!"

Dashawn was trying not to laugh.

"What's going on, Charlie?" Mrs. Burke asked.

I held up my new script. "I changed some of my lines. I didn't change anyone else's."

Mrs. Burke took the script. She looked at it, then she looked at me. Her face screwed up in a sort of smirk. I hoped that was a good sign. Maybe the Nice Gnome could be the Hilarious Gnome after all.

"You did this?" she asked me.

I nodded. "My friend Tommy helped me some because he types faster. If you want, we could print out copies for everyone."

She put my script under her arm. "Charlie, please go back to your old script. And Alex and Dashawn, please control yourselves."

"He's going to ruin the play!" Samantha said.

"He will not ruin the play," Mrs. Burke said. "No one ruins a play in Mrs. Burke's Empire. Now get back to rehearsing."

At the end of the school day, everyone was doing silent reading. "Charlie," Mrs. Burke said, "can I see you for a minute?"

I walked up to her desk.

She pointed to the printout sitting in front of her: my official new script with the Hilarious Gnome. "Why did you do this?"

"Um, I was thinking about the play and I thought that it might be a little better if my lines were different, but I knew you didn't have time so I decided I would see if I could make them better and…"

Mrs. Burke didn't say anything—she just kept looking at me over the top of her glasses.

I hate it when adults don't say anything. It's almost as bad as when they talk all the time, blah blah blah.

"And funnier," I added.

She looked at the script again.

"It's kind of funny," I said.

"Yes, it is," she said. "You did a lot of work on this."

"Uh-huh."

She handed it back to me. "You're not supposed to be funny in the play, Charlie. The Nice Gnome is not a wise guy. He is a helper."

"But he could be the Hilarious Gnome," I said. "He could still be good, but funnier. And nobody else would have to change anything."

"Charlie, if you don't do your part the way it's written, we're going to have problems. Do you want problems?"

"No," I said.

"Good. Neither do I."

Boogers.

13

Gnome Pants

Sunday afternoon I was finishing my homework in the kitchen, labeling continents and oceans on a map. I was thinking about what it would be like in Tierra del Fuego. It's this little piece of land way down at the bottom of South America. Part of it is in Chile—the country where Hector used to live. I wondered if he'd ever been there.

My mom came into the kitchen holding a piece of paper. "Charlie, I just got an e-mail from Mrs. Burke. It's a reminder to all the parents that you're supposed to bring in your costumes tomorrow. It says she sent a note home last week."

"Oh." I'd forgotten about it. "I guess it must be in my backpack."

Matt stuck his head through the doorway. "When's dinner?" he asked.

Mom kept talking to me. "Were you going to tell me about this? Don't you think we need to make a costume?"

"I guess."

"I'm starving," Matt said.

"When is the play?" Mom asked me. "Isn't it next Friday?"

"I think so," I said.

"Charlie!" she said. "We're going to have to make your costume tonight. What's the Nice Gnome supposed to wear?"

"I don't know," I said.

"I know!" Matt said. Suddenly he forgot he was starving. "He should wear a pointy red hat and pointy shoes and a pointy beard to match his pointy brain."

"That's enough, Matt," Mom said. "We'll just have to see what we can find around here."

"It's okay," I said. "You don't have to worry about it."

"Yes, I do," Mom said.

"I'll help," Matt said.

"No thank you," I said. The words "Matt" and "help" do not belong in the same sentence.

◆ ◆ ◆

The first thing we did was look at images of gnomes on the Internet. There were a lot of them.

"Hey, let's use this one." Matt pointed to a skinny creature all dressed in black and holding an electric guitar. "The Nasty Gnome."

Mom told me my gnome wasn't going to look like that. Or the ones with burning eyes and scowls and armor and swords. "I like these," she said, pointing to the ones with blue shirts, white beards, and red pointy hats.

Just what I was afraid of. "I don't," I said.

"Most of these gnomes

are wearing brown pants," Mom said, ignoring my comment. "You don't have any brown pants."

"Maybe I could wear jeans," I said. I was thinking a gnome who dressed exactly like I do would be a good idea.

"Wait," Mom said. "I know what we can use." She took me into her and Dad's bedroom and pulled out an old pair of shorts. "These don't fit your father anymore. Let's see how they look on you. They might be long enough for pants."

I put them on and looked in their big mirror. They were really baggy. The legs reached down almost all the way to my ankles.

"What are you doing?" the Squid asked, barging in.

"Working on Charlie's costume," Mom said. "We're trying to make him look like a gnome."

"I want to look like a gnome, too," she said.

"One gnome at a time," Mom said.

"I want to be a purple gnome," the Squid said.

Just then Dad walked in. "Hey, those are my shorts," he said.

"They're gnome pants now," Mom said. "You'll never fit in them again anyway."

I had to hold up the waist of Dad's shorts so they wouldn't fall off.

"I'm going to have to take them in," Mom said. "And we'll have to use a belt."

"Gnomes are fat," the Squid said. "Charlie should wear a pillow."

"Great idea, Mabel!" Mom said.

"I'll get one." Mabel grabbed a puffy pillow from the bed. Mom stuffed it into Dad's shorts.

Mom found an old blue sweatshirt of Matt's, and I pulled it on over the pillow. I was getting fatter by the second.

"He needs a beard," Dad said. "And I have just the thing." He left and came back with a really old mop—the little strands of rope looked sort of like shaggy hair.

"That's disgusting," Mom said.

"We can wash it," Dad said. He held it up to my chin.

It was the dumbest beard I had ever seen. It was actually pretty funny.

Matt came in to see what was going on. "He needs a pointy hat," he said.

I really didn't want a pointy hat, but before I knew it Mom had me in the car, trying to get to the fabric store before it closed. Mom bought some red felt for a hat. And purple felt for the Squid so she could be a purple gnome.

After dinner, Mom got out her sewing machine and sewed the hat. I put everything on except the beard.

"Go look in the mirror," Mom said. "It's fantastic!"

They all followed me into the hall and I stood in front of the long mirror. I held the mop up to my face.

When Ginger saw me, she growled and took a step back.

Ginger didn't like gnomes.

"You know, Charlie," Matt said. "I almost feel sorry for you."

"How come?" I asked.

"'Cause someone's going to bust you about that dorky hat and baggy pants."

"No they won't!" I shouted at him. "Stop it!"

"Cut it out, both of you," Dad said. He made Matt apologize and I said it was okay.

But it wasn't. What Matt said made me wonder if someone would give me a hard time. A lot of people would see the play. On Friday afternoon, our class would be on the stage at the monthly all-school meeting in the gym. We were going to dress up and talk about the play and ask people to come that night. I would have to wear my costume and say I was the Nice Gnome in front of everyone.

There were fifth graders like Larry Ladoux who would probably make fun of anything a fourth grader did. And there was Darren Thompson. He wasn't in my class this year, but he made fun of me and other kids all the time. And there were always three or four other boys who agreed with whatever Darren said because he was big and it seemed like a good idea to agree with him. He hadn't given me a wedgie this year, but he still might.

And then there was Tracy Hazlett. She was in Mrs. L.'s class with Tommy and Darren. I didn't think she would tease me, but I was afraid she might laugh at me. And I really didn't want Tracy Hazlett to laugh at me unless I was saying something funny.

Because I kind of liked her.

I don't want to talk about that anymore.

Except I was pretty sure Tracy might laugh at a fat Nice Gnome with baggy shorts and a pointy red hat and a mop for a beard.

Ha ha ha ha.

Dad took the mop so he could cut the stringy part off the handle and finish the beard, and Matt went to do his homework.

I followed my brother into his room. "Matt?"

"What?"

"I don't want to be the Nice Gnome. I don't want everyone to think I'm this goody-goody doofus or something. I hate the part, but I don't know how to get out of it. I tried to trade parts with someone, and then I tried changing the lines so they were better. But Mrs. Burke said no to everything."

Matt leaned back in his chair and stared at the ceiling. I could tell he was thinking. "Did you try messing up?" he asked.

"What do you mean?"

"If you mess up your part really badly, then maybe she'll have to find someone else to do it."

I thought about that. "Mrs. Burke gets mad at people who don't know their lines. What if she just kicks me out of the play?"

Matt shrugged. "She'd have to give you some part. Everybody always has a part in her plays."

"Do you really think it'll work? She could get mad."

"Desperate times call for desperate measures."

"I don't know," I said. Matt was pretty smart, but I still wasn't sure.

"Well, if it doesn't work, you're going to have to wear that dorky hat. And gnome shoes."

"I don't want gnome shoes!" I moaned. "I don't want to be a gnome!"

Matt grinned. "Well, you are a gnome, and you need gnome shoes."

14

You Look Like You Are Lost

Monday morning, the classroom was filled with paper bags and boxes and props to be used in the play. Everyone was showing off their costumes and the other stuff they'd brought. One of the parents had made hats for all the kids who were Mice in the Woods—baseball caps with little mouse ears on them and whiskers sticking off of the brim and a long tail trailing off the back of the hat. Sam Marchand had put on his cape with the awesome skull and was swirling it around.

"Can I see your costume?" Ellen Holmes asked me.

I pulled out the pointy cap and put it on.

"That's cute!" she said.

Boogers! I know she didn't mean it in a bad way, but I didn't want to be cute. I didn't want to be nice, either.

Which is why I did what I did.

I know I should've never listened to my older brother, but he seemed to have a magical power over me as strong as the Evil Sorcerer Kragon.

After lunch, Mrs. Burke told everyone to sit in a circle. "Today we're just going to go over our lines as quickly as we can," she said. "We're not going to stop for anything. If you get stuck, say, 'Line!' and I'll help you. But other than that, just keep going. No questions. No complaints. This way we'll find out where the problems are."

The scene in the castle went smoothly. The Prince and the Princess and their servants set off into the forest to search for the Magic Rabbit. When the Nice Gnome was supposed to speak, I didn't say anything.

"Charlie," Mrs. Burke said.

"Line!" I said.

Mrs. Burke seemed surprised, but she called it out: "You look like you are lost."

"You look like you are lost," I repeated.

Samantha was already rolling her eyes.

Dashawn was the Prince. He said, "We are lost. We'll never get out of these woods and find the Magic Talking Rabbit of Gorlandia."

I knew the next line.

But I didn't say anything.

"Charlie!" Mrs. Burke said.

"Line," I said.

Samantha's eyes looked like they were going to roll right out of her head.

Mrs. Burke gave me the line and I said it.

Samantha was so busy being disgusted with me that she forgot to say her next line.

Mrs. Burke waited.

"We have a long way to go," Samantha finally said. "We can't even get out of the woods and we have to find the Sorcerer's castle."

Mrs. Burke gave me a weird look. Maybe I'd gone too far. Matt was a bozo to think this plan would work. He didn't have to live in Mrs. Burke's Empire!

I decided I'd better stop messing up.

But now, I was confused. I honestly couldn't remember my next line. I had my script, and even though we weren't supposed to look at it, I did. But the pages were all out of order. So I just said, "Don't worry. We'll get there."

I knew it was wrong. So did everyone else.

"That's not your line!" Samantha hissed.

It got very quiet in the room. I stared down at the floor. When I snuck a glance at Mrs. Burke, she was glaring at me.

"Charlie doesn't know any of his lines," Samantha said.

Pow! Mrs. Burke snapped her fingers just once.

Everyone held their breath.

"Charlie," Mrs. Burke said, "you can go back to your desk for now. I'll read the Nice Gnome's lines."

I got up from the circle and went back to my desk. The class went on rehearsing with Mrs. Burke reading my part. I got a book out of my desk and pretended to read. But I couldn't. I was listening to everyone do their parts. Everyone was doing a good job.

Except for me.

I was not the Nice Gnome. Not anymore.

◆ ◆ ◆

When they finished rehearsing, Mrs. Burke told everyone to get ready to go home. Then she stood in the doorway.

"Charlie," she said. "Please come here."

"You're in so much trouble," Samantha said.

"Good luck, Charlie," Ellen Holmes whispered.

Hector cleaned off his glasses.

I got to the door and Mrs. Burke turned to the class. "Get your things together, everyone. I'll be watching." Then she motioned with her exploding bony fingers for me to follow her into the hall.

"Charlie," she said. "There is no excuse for what you have been doing."

I looked down the hallway to avoid looking at Mrs. Burke.

"You are ruining the play. You knew your part perfectly during the last rehearsal, but today you didn't even try. I'm very disappointed in you."

"I don't like my part," I mumbled. "I don't want to be the Nice Gnome."

"Why not?"

I shrugged. It was hard to explain. "Can't someone else do it?"

"Who?" she asked. "Who's going to do it?"

"Josh?"

"No, Josh has a part that's right for him. I don't

think anyone else could do the gnome part as well as you can. Or like I thought you could. This is your part, Charlie. What's the problem?"

I couldn't tell her that I didn't want to be the nice guy and wear a dorky costume. It would've been so much easier to be a bad guy, like the Evil Sorcerer Kragon. No one would've made fun of the bad guy.

"Charlie?"

"I wanted a different part."

"Why? The Nice Gnome is one of the most important roles in the play."

"But the Nice Gnome is just so…" I couldn't explain it to her.

"Tell me," she said, looking right at me. "Are you worried about being too nice?"

Boogers! How did she figure it out?

"Sort of," I mumbled.

"Charlie, you are not the Nice Gnome. You are just acting out the part. And besides, this play is not about you. It is about everyone working together on something. Your classmates are depending on you."

Now I felt really crummy.

She gave my shoulder a little squeeze. "You have three days to turn this around, and I suggest you start doing it right now. Now get back into class and get ready to go home."

I turned to head back into our room.

"Charlie," Mrs. Burke said. "I don't need you to be a perfect Nice Gnome. I just need you to be a fairly friendly one who knows his lines."

When we lined up to go home, Hector tapped me on the shoulder. "If you need help with your lines, let me know."

"Thanks," I said.

15

The Biggest Bozo on the Planet

The Squid talked all the way home from the bus stop. "We're going to see your play on Friday night. Mrs. Diaz told our whole class we should see it. She gave us a handout so we could remember by giving it to our parents."

That didn't make me feel any better.

When I walked in and Ginger jumped on me for the millionth time, that made me feel even worse.

Matt wasn't in the kitchen.

"Would someone else please walk Ginger?" I yelled.

I heard Matt call from his bedroom, "No!"

"I'll walk her," the Squid said.

"You're still too little," I said.

"No, I'm not," she said. "I grew even more. I can walk her. I'll even do it for free!"

I thought about Mabel walking Ginger all the way around the block. It was too far. And what if they ran into Lovey-Doodle? Or the dumb cats and the cat lady? Or even worse, the squirrels? Plus, Mom always said Matt and I weren't supposed to let Mabel go *anywhere* unless we were with her.

"Please, Charlie! I can do it. I'll just walk her down to the corner and back."

I thought about that. It seemed like a pretty good idea. If Ginger pooped quickly like she did the other day, they could just come right back. I could look out the front door and check on them. If Ginger didn't do her business, then I'd just have to take her on her regular walk.

"Just to the end of the block?" I asked.

"Yes!"

"And if she poops, you'll pick it up?"

She frowned. "I don't want to pick up the poop."

"Okay, I'll pay you a dollar if she poops and you pick it up."

Her eyebrows went up. "A whole dollar?"

"But only if she poops and you pick it up, because if she doesn't, I'll still have to walk her."

The Squid twisted her mouth around, thinking. "Okay, for a whole dollar I'll do it."

"Okay," I said. "It's a deal."

"Can I have the dollar now?"

All this time, Ginger was barking and jumping around. I took an old plastic shopping bag from the drawer and handed it to the Squid.

"Get the dollar," she said.

I ran upstairs to my room and got a dollar out of my desk. I hurried back and held it out for the Squid.

"Leave it on the table," she said, "and don't touch it." She'd already taken the leash down and put it on Ginger's collar.

"Ginger, sit!" I said.

She sat at the door and looked up at us. Her tail was wagging like it would fall off.

"If she pulls too much," I said, "just give her a big tug and yell, 'Ginger, no!'"

"Okay, I'm ready." The Squid was holding onto the leash with both hands.

I watched them walk down the driveway, with Ginger sniffing and straining at the leash. "No, Ginger, no!" the Squid shouted.

They zigzagged down the sidewalk. I hoped everything would go okay. Every few seconds, I stuck my head out the front door to see how she was doing.

Matt came into the kitchen and saw me standing in the doorway.

"Where's Mabel?" he asked.

"Walking Ginger," I said.

"What?" Matt looked at me like I was crazy.

"Mabel's walking Ginger."

"Why?"

"She said she wanted to, so I let her."

"You're an idiot," Matt said. "Mabel can't control that crazy dog."

"It'll be okay," I said. "She's just walking to the end of the street and I'm checking on her real often."

"You'd better go help her," Matt said. He started for the refrigerator. Then he saw the money on the table. "Whose is this?"

"Mabel's."

"Wait a minute! Did you *pay* Mabel to walk Ginger?"

"So?"

"Charlie, that was mega-stupid."

"No, it wasn't!" I said. "It's going to be okay."

Just then, we heard someone running up the driveway. The Squid burst through the kitchen door holding the leash.

"Help!" she said. "Ginger got away! She pulled too hard and the leash didn't work!"

"Oh man." Matt gave me a Buck Mcson electron stare. "Mom and Dad are going to kill all of us!"

"It's not my fault!" The Squid's eyes filled with tears. "Ginger crossed the street and I was only supposed to go to the end of the block, so I couldn't run after her."

Matt was really mad, and the Squid was crying.

And I was the biggest bozo on the planet.

"Let's go," Matt said. He slipped on his jacket. "We've got to find her."

We opened the door and headed down the porch steps.

And Mom pulled in the driveway.

Mom drove slowly down the street with Matt in the front and the Squid and me in the back. We all looked out the windows, trying to catch sight of Ginger.

Mom turned the corner at the end of our block. "This is the way she went, Mabel?"

"Uh-huh," Mabel said, still sniffling. "I couldn't stop her."

"It's okay, sweetie," Mom said. "We'll find her." She didn't even look at me. It made me feel even worse.

We drove around our block twice, then Mom headed toward the next street over. When Matt had told Mom what had happened and Mabel had tried to explain, I hadn't said anything. I knew it was all my fault.

It was very quiet in the car. I just kept praying we would see Ginger. If she was lost, I didn't know what I'd do.

After about half an hour Mom pulled into a driveway and turned around. "Well, we've done what we can. We'll just have to go home. I'll call around to our neighbors and ask if anyone has seen her."

"But we have to find her!" the Squid wailed.

"We will, we will," Mom said. She was saying that because she was the mom, but I could tell she was worried, too.

When we got to our house, Dad's car was in the driveway. Now I was going to be in trouble with everyone.

"I want Ginger!" Mabel whimpered. "I wish I could help get her back."

Everybody went inside, but I stayed in the car. What if we never found Ginger? If only it was like in the play and we had the Nice Gnome or the Magic Rabbit to help us. There had to be a way to—

Suddenly I knew what to do. And I was the only one who could do it. Why hadn't I thought of it before?

I jumped out of the car and ran to the sidewalk in front of our house. I put my fingers in my mouth and blew.

I blew and blew and blew until my mouth hurt.

I waited and listened. But I didn't hear anything but a car honking somewhere.

Even my special Uncle Ron whistle wasn't working. Ginger was gone.

I tried one last time, just to make sure.

Then I heard a bark.

I looked down the street, in the direction of the Gritzbachs' yard. A big brown and black dog was running toward me as fast as she could.

"Ginger!" I knelt down to catch her and she knocked me over. I hugged her and she licked my face.

"You dumb dog." I nuzzled her furry neck. I didn't care if she was a dumb dog. She was home.

When I opened the back door, Ginger ran in and the Squid let out her excited squeal. Mom covered her mouth and looked like she was going to cry. Dad put his arm around her. Even Matt, who'd said he only wanted a python, got down and gave Ginger a hug.

"How'd you find her?" Dad asked.

"I whistled," I said.

"Only Charlie can whistle like that," the Squid

said. "She only comes for Charlie."

In the middle of our celebration, the phone in the kitchen rang. My mom picked it up. "Hello? Yes... Hi, Connie... Yes, she's home... Oh no, really? I'm so sorry... Oh, good." Then she laughed. "No. Don't you touch it. I'll send Charlie down right away."

She hung up the phone. "That was Mrs. Gritzbach."

Uh-oh.

"She called to see if Ginger was home. She said Ginger had been in their yard and she had, uh..."

"Answered the call of nature?" Dad asked.

"Yes. Right in front of their house. But Mr. Gritzbach isn't home yet. So, Charlie, if you hurry down there, you can clean it up before he gets back."

"Okay." I grabbed a plastic bag from the drawer.

"See you later, Poopmeister," Matt said.

I was so happy to have Ginger back, I didn't mind being the Poopmeister.

"That's *Master* Poopmeister to you," I said, heading out the door.

◆ ◆ ◆

I got the mess cleaned up before Mr. Gritzbach saw it, but I don't have to tell you I got a lecture when I got back.

Actually, I got a bunch of lectures.

I got a lecture from my mom.

I got a lecture from my dad.

They both made me apologize to the Squid. I apologized. And I meant it.

I figured I wouldn't ask about watching *Buck Meson* for a couple of weeks. It seemed like a bad idea.

Matt told me it was the dumbest thing I had ever done. "And for someone who's a total dorkhead," he said, "that is really, really dumb."

Only the Squid stood up for me. "It's not fair," she said to Mom and Dad. "It's not Charlie's fault the leash didn't work."

"The leash is not the point," Dad said. "It was Charlie's responsibility to walk the dog." He looked at me. "You knew Mabel was too little."

I knew Dad was right, so I couldn't argue.

Ginger just licked my face. She wasn't mad at me.

That's why you have a dog.

16

That Kid with the Beard

We had rehearsals on Tuesday and Wednesday afternoon. Things went pretty well, but I was still having trouble with my long speech. Tommy and Hector went over my lines with me after rehearsal. Wednesday night I even asked Matt to help me practice.

"This is a dumb play," he said.

"You don't have to tell me that," I said.

"Okay," he said, "I won't tell you it's a dumb play, even though it is." But then he read all the lines really well, so I began to think he'd just said it was dumb because he had to, since he was my older brother.

Thursday was the day for the dress rehearsal. That morning when I got into class, everyone was crowded around Crystal Medeiros's desk. There was an animal cage on it, and Killer was inside. Kids from my class were on their knees, peering in and sticking their fingers through the mesh wire.

"Can I hold Killer?" Alex asked. "Just for a minute?"

Everyone chimed in, all wanting to do the same thing.

Mrs. Burke was watching. "I don't think we should take the rabbit out during class."

"My dad said I could take him out of the cage once or twice," Crystal said, "but I have to hold him. You can pet him, though."

"Please, Mrs. Burke?" Trevor asked.

"All right, then," Mrs. Burke said. "But I want everyone to sit on the floor and let Crystal bring the rabbit around. In five minutes, Killer goes back in his cage."

Crystal took Killer out of the cage. She held him

tightly to her body and let everyone pat his head and side. He had hilarious long ears that drooped down the side of his head and his nose was twitching like something was tickling it.

That afternoon, Mrs. Burke sent the kids with costumes to the girls' and boys' rooms down the hall to get dressed. Mrs. Berman, Lydia's mom, came in to help. She kept knocking on the boys' bathroom door to tell us to hurry up.

Some people can't help being parents, even when they're in school.

When I came out of the bathroom, Mrs. L.'s class was coming back from the library. Darren Thompson stopped and pointed at me. Oh great.

"Looky, looky, looky!" he said. "It's a little pointy-headed troll."

I walked on past the line of kids, ignoring him.

"Hi, Charlie," said Tommy, giving me a thumbs-up. "Cool costume."

Tracy Hazlett was staring at me.

124

"What are you?" she asked.

"The…um…Nice Gnome," I muttered.

She nodded and smiled.

I thought I was going to throw up a little.

We had almost made it to safety inside the gym when Larry Ladoux, the mean fifth grader, saw us. "Look at the dorky outfits," he said. "Especially that kid with the beard."

"Everyone into the gym!" called Mrs. Burke. "Line up in front of the stage."

Ms. Bromley, the art teacher, had helped the crew finish the set, and it was on the stage. When Mr. Turchin, the school custodian, turned on the colored lights overhead, it made everything look really beautiful.

We went through the whole play. It took almost an hour because we had to stop four or five times.

General Shuler, (our new PE teacher is so strict I call him General Shuler, the Intergalactic Supreme Commander of Soccer Balls) had had to cancel his gym classes. He watched the whole thing with his arms folded across his chest and his eyebrows squinched down. He would've made a great Angry Gnome.

Maybe because everyone was so excited, people kept making mistakes. There was so much noise people couldn't hear Mrs. Burke's snapping fingers. She clapped her hands and called, "Pay attention, everyone!"

Then it was time for the castle to be moved, but Joey and Alex weren't ready.

"Where's the stage crew?" she shouted. "Alex! Joey! Where are you?"

I ran back behind the set. They were down on their knees looking at Killer in his cage.

"You guys," I said. "Hurry up. You're supposed to be moving the castle. Mrs. Burke is getting mad."

Alex got up and looked around, like he didn't know where the castle was.

"Over there!" I pointed to a corner of the stage behind the curtain. I'd read the dumb play so many times, I knew exactly where the castle was supposed to be.

◆ ◆ ◆

When I got home, I stopped in my tracks in front of the back steps.

The Squid was right behind me. "Look, Charlie!" she squealed. "It's you!"

I couldn't believe it.

A big plastic gnome was standing on the top step. It had an electric cord on it, so you could plug it in and it would light up.

I wondered if Matt had put it there to terrorize me.

"Matt!" I yelled.

He stuck his head out the door and saw the gnome. "Hey, where'd that come from?"

"You didn't put it there?"

"No," he said. "But I wish I had."

Then I saw the envelope taped to the gnome's head. It had "Charlie" written on it.

There was a card inside.

I opened it and read the note.

Dear Charlie,

Thank you so much for helping me with Lovey-Doodle. I spoke with your mother and understand you're in a big play. Since you're the Nice Gnome, I thought it might be fun for you to have one for your room. You can use it as a night-light!

Many thanks,
Sharon Lapidus and Lovey-Doodle

"The Nice Gnome's cousin!" said Matt.

"I wish I had a gnome," the Squid said.

◆ ◆ ◆

That night I set up the gnome in the corner of my room and plugged it in. With the other lights turned off, it glowed like one of those radioactive aliens Buck Meson always paralyzes with his electron stare.

I stood in front of the mirror over my chest of drawers, practicing my part. I kept saying the last line to my big speech over and over again: "Follow your heart, follow your heart, follow your heart."

Matt came in the room. He had a bag and a stack of newspapers under his arm.

"What's that?" I asked.

"The Nice Gnome might have to be nice," Matt said, "but he can still be cool."

"What do you mean?"

"Follow me."

I followed him down the stairs, out the kitchen door, and into the open garage. He spread the newspapers on the concrete floor.

"What are you doing?" I asked.

He reached in the bag and pulled out a pair of dirty white sneakers. "Size five shoes for the Nice Gnome," he said. "These are my old ones, but gnomes have big feet."

"They're white," I said. "They should be brown."

"No, they shouldn't," he said.

"What do you mean?"

Then he reached in the bag and pulled out a can of spray paint. "The Guh-nice Guh-nome shouldn't have brown pointy shoes. The Guh-nice Guh-nome needs golden shoes."

He put the shoes down on the newspaper and held out the can. "Be my guest!"

I looked at him. "Really?"

"Really!" he said.

I took the can and sprayed Matt's old sneakers until they were completely gold.

They looked amazing.

"This is so awesome," I said.

"Awesome shoes," Matt said. "Awesome gnome."

At the all-school meeting the next afternoon, we filed up onto the stage in our costumes. I was still a little nervous about being a gnome, with my dad's shorts flapping around and my beard and pointy hat. But there were so many kids dressed up in all sorts of odd-looking outfits, I didn't really stick out.

As I came out on stage with the rest of the class, Ellen Holmes was standing at the microphone, ready to tell everyone that they should come to the play.

And then the Squid saw me.

She was sitting up toward the very front, wearing her purple gnome hat. Before Mrs. Diaz could stop her, my sister stood and said, "Charlie's the Nice Gnome. He's a really Nice Gnome, and he's wearing the gold shoes that Matt gave him."

Everybody cracked up. I heard Tommy hoot. Hector poked me. Samantha rolled her eyes.

Brady Bernhart, a crazy first grader with this weird croaky voice, yelled, "Cool shoes, Charlie!"

17

A Million Chairs

Friday night Dad came home early and brought Chinese take-out for dinner. I had to be at the school at six o'clock, so we ate quickly. At five forty-five we all got in the car. I carried my costume in a bag, but the Squid wore her purple T-shirt and purple gnome hat.

Mom took the script in the car and kept reading my lines aloud to make sure I knew them.

"Stop it, Mom," Matt said. "You're just making the Guh-nice Guh-nome guh-nervous."

"I agree," said my dad.

So did I.

I could still feel that last egg roll sitting on top of my stomach. And for some reason the tune to the *Buck Meson* theme song kept playing in my head.

When we got to the school, I was even more nervous. My mom hugged me and said, "Break a leg!"

"What?" I said.

"It's what actors say for good luck," she said.

Actors are weird.

Mr. Turchin had set out a million chairs for the audience. A lot of parents were already there, and a bunch of brothers and sisters and babies and grandmothers and granddads. I saw kids from other classes, too.

I went down to our classroom, where we were all supposed to meet. Mrs. Berman and a couple of other parents were helping kids get the costumes ready. Crystal carried in Killer's cage and set it down in the corner. Alex was running all over as usual. The Prince's Servant, Hector, had on a fancy jacket and one of his dad's bow ties.

Mrs. Burke was walking around, eating from a plastic container of salad.

I got dressed quickly and put on my beard. Mrs. Berman helped me stuff the pillow into my Gnome pants.

"Line up!" Mrs. Burke said. "It's time for us to go." She led us down the hallway, eating salad as she went. We followed her all the way to the gym and around to the back of the stage.

She put down her salad container and gathered us around. "Listen, all of you citizens of Mrs. Burke's Empire. Your job is to pay attention and play your part in the best way you can. Tonight we're all going to work together and create something wonderful."

While she was talking, I saw Alex way at the back, on his knees by Killer's cage. When Mrs. Burke finished, I went over to see what he was doing.

He had opened the cage door a little and was feeding Killer a piece of lettuce from Mrs. Burke's salad.

"Leave the rabbit alone, you wacko," I whispered.

"It's my job," Alex said. "I'm in charge of Killer."

"Just make sure you close the cage," I said.

"Okay, okay." Alex closed the cage, then ran off on his crazy legs.

Off to the side I saw Dashawn in his Prince's costume. His crown was sitting to one side on his head and he was frowning.

"What's wrong?" I asked.

"My stomach feels weird."

"I know what you mean," I said. "I feel the same way."

Dashawn tried to smile, but he looked really nervous.

"It's okay," I told him. "You'll do great."

He nodded. "Thanks."

"Everyone in positions!" Mrs. Burke said. "I'll say a few words and then Ellen can introduce the play. Break a leg, class!"

All the kids in the first scene walked on the stage. Trevor David, the King, lay down across a couple of chairs with a blanket over him. Taleea Dawson, the Queen, stood next to him. The King's Advisors took their places on one side of the chairs with the Wise Woman, Lydia Berman, on the other. We could hear Mrs. Burke talking in front of the curtain.

"Welcome, everyone, to our play, *The Sorcerer's Castle*. We're so glad you're here. We've worked very hard together and I think you're going to enjoy yourselves. Now, let the show begin!"

The colored lights were shining down on the stage and everything looked really amazing. Fancy orchestra music was playing on the loud speaker.

It made me excited. And even more nervous.

I really didn't want to mess up in front of all those people.

I peeked out and saw Tommy and Matt sitting next to each other in the front row. Mabel was on the other side of Matt. I couldn't see my parents— they must have been further back.

Tracy Hazlett was sitting in the front row, too. The egg roll in my stomach did a somersault.

When Ellen Holmes went out in front of the

curtain, everyone got quiet. "Once upon a time," she said in a loud voice, "in the land of Gorlandia, the King had fallen ill. No one knew what to do."

Alexandra pulled the curtain, and everyone applauded. The play had started.

I couldn't really see the action on the stage, but I could hear everything. When the Wise Woman mentioned the Magic Rabbit, I knew that the Prince and Princess were supposed to make their entrance.

"Dashawn!" Samantha said. "Hurry up. It's our turn!"

Dashawn the Prince just stood there holding his stomach. "I can't," he said.

"It's okay," I whispered. "Go ahead."

"I mean, I feel like—"

And then he turned his head away from me and threw up on the floor.

18

No Idea What to Say

Four or five other kids were standing around, and they all screamed and took a step back. Dashawn didn't seem to know what to do. Mrs. Burke was on the other side of the stage. I looked around and spotted the box where Mr. Turchin puts lost stuff. I ran over, grabbed an old T-shirt from the box, and handed it to Dashawn so he could wipe his face.

Samantha had already gone on stage without him. She turned back and whispered, "Dashawn, hurry up!"

I heard some people in the audience laughing.

I patted Dashawn on the back. "You're okay," I

said. "You can do it. Go out and say, 'I'll do whatever I can to save my father.'"

Dashawn nodded, handed me the shirt, then wobbled out onto the stage next to Samantha.

I was left holding an old T-shirt with Dashawn's dinner on it. It was like holding a bag of Ginger's call of nature. You just had to do your job and move on. I dropped it in the corner and watched the play.

Dashawn went over and put his hand on Trevor's head.

Please don't throw up on him, I thought.

"I'll do whatever I can to save my father," Dashawn said, then covered his mouth.

Samantha opened her arms like she was an opera singer or something. "So will I!" she crowed.

Some more people laughed. I could see Samantha was a little surprised.

But the show went on.

Everyone backstage was avoiding the place where Dashawn had thrown up. Even Mrs. Berman wouldn't go near it. People on that side had no way to get on stage. Someone had to do something. I scooted down the steps at the side of the stage. My dad's shorts started to slip down, so I pulled them back up over the pillow.

"Mr. Turchin!" I called, hoping the people in the audience wouldn't notice me.

"What're you doin' here, Charlie?" he asked. "Aren't you the Nice Gnome?"

"Yeah," I said, "but Dashawn threw up all over the place and I'm afraid everyone else is going to throw up, too."

"Be right there." He slipped out the side door of the gym and disappeared. I'd never seen Mr. Turchin move that fast.

Just as I turned to go up the stairs, I heard the Squid yell, "There's Charlie! He's the Nice Gnome!"

I just kept going.

When I got backstage, the next scene had already started. The Prince and Princess were already lost in the woods.

It was time for the Nice Gnome to show up.

Samantha shrieked, "We'll never get out of here!"

I rushed to the edge of the curtain, stopped to adjust my beard, then took a big breath and walked out on stage.

Tommy and the Squid applauded. A couple of other people joined in. I looked at the audience, and for a second, I completely freaked out.

There were a million people out there, and they were all looking at me!

Maybe *I* was going to throw up.

"Excuse me," I said in my best Nice Gnome voice. As soon as I spoke, something in me calmed down.

Everything in the scene went almost perfectly. We met the Fox, the only character who spoke in rhyme. Once Robby got one of his lines a little mixed up, but I nodded and he went on.

By the time we walked off the stage so the crew could change the set, Mr. Turchin had already mopped the place where Dashawn had thrown up. It hardly smelled at all.

At the beginning of the next scene, Joey Alvares pushed the button for the swampy, creepy sound effects. Samantha and Dashawn and I walked across the stage to go to the swamp. The two of them were supposed to yell when Josh the Slimy Snake of the Swamp slithered out.

But instead of yelling, Samantha let out a high-pitched scream. Dashawn just stared at her. She'd never done that before. Josh slithered around on stage. Samantha was supposed to say, "A snake! Is it poisonous?"

She stopped screaming, but then she just stood there and stared out at the audience.

Then she looked offstage at Mrs. Burke, who was leafing through the script trying to find where we were in the play.

Samantha started to shake a little. Her bottom lip was trembling and I could tell she was about to cry. For once, Samantha Grunsky had no idea what to say.

I knew her line, but I was too far away to whisper it to her.

Dashawn wasn't going to say anything—he was probably still afraid of what might come out of his mouth.

Josh was busy being a snake, hissing. But I didn't think he could hiss forever.

"All of you are probably wondering," I blurted out, "if this snake is poisonous. Let's just ask it. 'Are you poisonous, O Slimy Snake'?"

"Yesssss, I am," Josh said, "but I've lost my rattle!"

Then he hissed some more.

Samantha gave a little nod, then said her next line. "Please don't bite us."

And the play went on.

I don't think anybody in the audience really knew that anything was wrong.

When we walked off the stage at the end of the scene, Josh said, "Good job, Charlie!"

Samantha didn't say anything. Maybe she was upset that Charlie Bumpers, the idiot gnome, had saved her.

We got through the desert scene without a problem, except for when the two ends of the camel got separated. While I was trying to get Tricia and Sarah back together, my beard fell off. I put it back on, but it wouldn't stay. Suddenly Hector was at my side.

"Help me, Prince's Servant," I said. "My beard is falling off."

"Of course, Nice Gnome," he said. He reattached my beard, then helped the camel get together again.

The audience was dying with laughter. When the camel was back in one piece, it bowed and people applauded.

It was almost time for my big speech, right before the Prince and Princess go away to the Sorcerer's Castle.

Dashawn said his line: "But Nice Gnome, you can't leave us here."

Samantha said hers: "Yes, Nice Gnome. We can't do this without you."

And then I said, "I'm sorry, but this is as far…"

I started again. "This is as far as…"

Everyone on stage just stared at me. No one knew my lines. Not even Samantha Grunsky, Princess of Everything.

I looked offstage for Mrs. Burke. She wasn't where she'd been standing before. I could feel sweat trickling down my back.

I was all alone. And I was messing up.

And then I spotted Tommy. He was crouching right below the stage, holding a script. "This is as far as I can go," he whispered.

I repeated the line, but I couldn't remember the next one.

"You know what you need to know," Tommy whispered.

As soon as I'd said that line, I started to remember. "Look at all the friends you have now. They all have special gifts, and they all want to help. I can't go any farther—my Gnomish nature forbids it. But you will be fine. Just, just…"

What was next?

I looked down. Tommy had already gone back to his seat. The audience was quiet, waiting.

"Just, just…"

And then I saw my brother Matt pointing to his chest.

"Heart!" I said. "Just follow your heart! Farewell!"

Everyone started applauding. Dazed, I bowed and walked off stage.

19

Mwa-ha-ha-ha!

Alex and Joey and Alexandra pushed the Sorcerer's castle back onto the stage. It was time for the big scene where the Prince and Princess get the Magic Rabbit. I'd finished my part, so I was having fun watching everyone else.

Sam came over and stood beside me. "I know I'm going to mess up."

"No, you aren't," I said. "But if you do, just do your laugh a lot."

Sam smiled a little. "Okay. Mwa-ha-ha-ha."

"Mwa-ha-ha-ha."

I gave him a high five and he walked onto the stage.

No one forgot any lines. Every time Sam did his laugh, the audience laughed, too. He started laughing longer and louder than he should have, but I couldn't blame him. I whispered his best line to myself as he spoke: "You horrible people! My plans are ruined! My dreams are ruined! I am ruined!"

Everyone cheered. Sam had done a great job. Cory, one of the Sorcerer's Assistants, ran around to the other side of the stage. He was supposed to come right back with Killer, the Magic Rabbit.

But he didn't.

The next thing I knew, Cory was next to me holding the cage.

It was empty.

"Killer's gone!"

Lydia's mother gasped.

"Killer?" She looked around her feet like someone had let loose a rat or snake or something that was going to bite her.

I looked over at Alex.

"I guess I didn't close the cage very well," he gulped.

On the other side of the stage, I could see Mrs. Burke and a bunch of kids crawling around on the floor, looking for the rabbit. All the kids on my side joined in the search. "Killer! Killer!" they called out. "Where are you?"

Everyone on the stage was just standing around, not sure what to do. They needed Cory to come back with the Magic Rabbit.

"Mwa-ha-ha-ha!" Sam's laugh was almost a shout now. "Where's my assistant? Mwa-ha-ha-ha-ha!"

Before I could say anything to Cory, he ran out on stage holding the empty cage.

"The Magic Rabbit is missing!" he said.

This definitely wasn't in the script. No one knew what to do.

"Mwa-ha-ha-ha!" Sam said, but not quite so loud.

Some kids in the audience started to giggle.

Then Dashawn said, "You must find the Magic Rabbit, or our father will die."

That wasn't in the script either!

"Mwa-ha-ha," Sam said weakly.

The actors looked at each other, not knowing what else to say.

Backstage, everyone was still crawling around looking for Killer.

The play was ruined.

And then I figured it out.

I ran to the back of the stage and climbed over the gym mats and the desks and chairs and the preschool slide. I saw the little kindergarten desk where Mrs. Burke had left her salad container. Someone had knocked it off onto the floor.

And there was Killer, munching away on the spilled salad.

Very carefully, I lifted the rabbit up and cradled him in my arms. I climbed back over all the stuff and ran to the side of the stage. The scene hadn't changed. Dashawn and Sam and Cory and everybody else were still standing around and staring at each other.

Sam made up a line, hoping to find a way to get to the next scene. "If the Rabbit is lost," he said, "then the King will die. Mwa-ha-ha."

I walked out onto the stage holding Killer. Everyone turned and looked at me.

I hadn't thought about what to say, but then the exact right line came to me. I gave Sam the Buck Meson electron stare and said, "You think the King will die? I DON'T THINK SO!"

Half of the kids on stage burst into laughter. Samantha looked over like she wanted to strangle me. I heard my brother's high-pitched cackle. Tommy whooped and shouted, "Buck Meson! I don't think so!"

Crystal Medeiros, the Blind Owl, came on and took the cage away from Cory, which was a little hard for her to do with the big owl's wings attached to her arms. She held out the cage to me and I slipped Killer inside. Then I closed the latch and jiggled it to make sure it was locked.

I knew I had to get out of the scene so they could finish the play. "I feel weak from being in this evil place," I said. "I must answer the call of nature." There was more laughter in the audience. I bowed and headed off the stage.

Everyone applauded.

I looked across the stage and saw Mrs. Burke.

She was laughing and clapping, too.

The last scene went really well. The Prince and Princess took the Magic Rabbit back to their Kingdom, and the Magic Rabbit whispered in the Queen's ear how to make the King a healing tea with the magic tea leaves he had brought. After the King was cured, the Prince and Princess and all the Advisors shouted, "Hurrah! Long live the King!" Alexandra pulled the curtains, and the audience went wild.

We all arranged ourselves in a line like Mrs. Burke had shown us, and the curtain opened again. We bowed together, then each of us took a bow by ourselves. When it came time for me, I thought the applause seemed a little louder. In the front row, Tommy and Matt both were yelling, "I don't think so! I don't think so!"

I was the Nice Gnome. The Awesome Nice Gnome. It felt pretty good.

Finally the clapping and cheering died down, and we filed off the stage. All the kids were giving each other high fives. Some of the parents had brought cookies and juice. One smart dad had brought three pizzas. If he'd been really smart, he would've brought five. I ate Dashawn's slice because he said he wasn't hungry. Kids crowded around the rabbit cage, and Crystal let everyone feed Killer little bits of lettuce from Mrs. Burke's salad.

I gave Hector a pat on the back. "You did a great job! You saved my beard, and you didn't mess up like I did."

"You? Mess up?" He grinned. "I don't think so!"

Then Sam came over. At the very same time we both said, "Mwa-ha-ha-ha!"

And then we realized that someone else was laughing with us. "Mwa-ha-ha-ha!"

We turned around. It was Mrs. Burke.

She put one arm around my shoulder and the other one around Sam's. "My Nice Evil Sorcerer and my Evil Nice Gnome. I'm proud of both of you."

And then we all laughed. One more time. Together.

"MWA-HA-HA-HA!"

Don't miss the first book in the
Charlie Bumpers series—
Charlie Bumpers vs. the Teacher of the Year.

And coming up next, the third book—

Turn the page for a sneak peek…

1
Tons of Candy

"What are you wearing for Halloween?" Tommy asked.

"I don't know," I said. There were only twelve days to Halloween, and I hadn't decided what I wanted to be.

Tommy Kasten's my best friend. He and I were leaning against the wall in the gym during recess. It was raining too hard to go outside. There were two different kickball games going, a basketball game, and some kids skipping rope. It was so loud with everyone yelling and screaming, Tommy and I could barely hear ourselves think. For a few minutes we watched everyone else run around.

Mr. Shuler, our gym teacher was watching, too. I could tell by the look on his face that he didn't like all these kids crowded in his gym.

"Maybe I'll go as Mr. Shuler," I said. "That would be scary."

"Ha!" Tommy said. "I'm going as a werewolf. I've got some fangs to put in my mouth, and I'm going to glue hair all over my hands and face."

"Your mom's actually going to let you glue hair on yourself?" I asked.

"I hope so," Tommy said.

"That will be great. But I just can't think of anything this year."

"Well, you'd better figure something out pretty soon," he said. "Don't forget about the costume contest. The winner gets ten free movie tickets."

"I know."

There was going to be a costume contest at school the day of Halloween, and I wanted to win. Then Tommy and I could go to the movie five times together. Or maybe I would take someone else, too.

Like Hector, who sits next to me in Mrs. Burke's fourth-grade class.

"You want to come to my house for trick-or-treating?" I asked.

"I'll have to bring Carla if I come," Tommy said.

Carla is Tommy's little sister. She's in first grade, just like my sister Mabel, and they're best friends, too. My dad calls Mabel "Squirt," but I call her "the Squid" because it's funnier.

"I know," I said. "I always have to take the Squid around. We could do it together."

"I guess," Tommy said. "The only problem with Carla is she slows me down. I can never get to as many houses as I want. And when our mom or dad goes with us, they stop and talk to the grown-ups handing out the candy. It's worse than going to the supermarket with them. It takes forever."

"Exactly!" I said.

"Too bad we can't go by ourselves," Tommy said.

"And it's too bad we can't go in a neighborhood where the houses are really big and everyone hands out large candy bars."

"Right!" said Tommy, getting more excited. "The bigger the houses, the bigger the candy bars! Then maybe we'd have to carry extra bags for when the first ones got filled up. That would be stupendous."

"Terrific!" I said.

"Stupific!" Tommy said.

"Stupific!" I repeated. "That's hilarious."

"Stupific!" we both said at the same time.

"Wait!" Tommy said. "Maybe your brother Matt could take Carla and Mabel around, and we could go to a different neighborhood by ourselves!"

"Maybe," I said. But I wondered if Matt would really take two first graders out trick-or-treating. Anyway, the Squid usually wanted to do things with me.

"Hey!" Alex MacLeod ran up, bouncing a ball a million miles an hour. He's a nice guy, but very hyper. Very, very hyper.

"What are you guys doing for Halloween?" Alex asked, still bouncing.

"Trick-or-treating," Tommy said. "Duh."

Alex lost the ball and ran to retrieve it. When he bounced it back our way, I caught it and held on to it. He didn't seem to notice.

"You wanna come to my house?" he asked. "I'm going to have a sleepover. We'll go out trick-or-treating in my neighborhood, then watch horror movies. It'll be great."

Tommy and I looked each other. A dream come true. We knew where Alex lived—his house was really big, and his neighborhood was full of other big houses. Every one of them was probably loaded with tons of candy.

Carla and Mabel the Squid wouldn't be there. Tons of candy! Heaven on earth on Halloween!

Tommy and I smiled at each other.

"Sure," I said.

"How many bags should we bring?" Tommy asked.

"As many as you want," Alex said. "It's going to be awesome. And I'm going to get some really scary movies."

"I love horror movies," Tommy said.

"I hope we can get *The Shrieking Skull*," Alex said. "It's the scariest horror movie ever!"

"Fantastic!" Tommy said.

"Ask your parents if you can come," Alex said. "We'll eat candy and pizza until we throw up and then watch movies and scream like crazy."

"Stupific!" Tommy said.

"Super stupific," I said.

Halloween with friends. Lots of candy. All of it was really stupific.

Except for one thing.

I HATE horror movies.

BILL HARLEY is the author of the award-winning middle reader novels *The Amazing Flight of Darius Frobisher* and *Night of the Spadefoot Toads*. He is also a storyteller, musician, and writer who has been writing and performing for kids and families for more than twenty years. Harley is the recipient of Parents' Choice and ALA awards, as well as two Grammy Awards. He lives in Massachusetts.

www.billharley.com

ADAM GUSTAVSON has illustrated many books for children, including *Lost and Found*; *The Blue House Dog*; *Mind Your Manners, Alice Roosevelt!*; and *Snow Day!* He lives in New Jersey.

www.adamgustavson.com